MW00427692

Stars of the Now

By Brian P. Fox

Copyright 2013 Brian P. Fox

Published by Polite Society

Printed by CreateSpace

If you would like to share this book with another person, please purchase
an additional copy for each recipient. If you're reading this book and did
not purchase it, or it was not purchased for your use only, then please
return to Amazon.com or other retail outlets and purchase your own
copy. Thank you for respecting the hard work of this author.

Table of Contents

Bubble

Streetlamps shine soft pools of light onto the empty street ahead of me – tiny, spotlighted, theater stages, under the canopied greenery, bubbling out of the blue-black, small town night. My little sports car, humming with Japanese precision, slices through the silence as I race through the bright, cone shaped pockets. Squealing the tires perfectly around a corner, I leave crescent shaped arcs of rubber on the concrete beneath us. Silhouettes of moms and pops, framed by the blue glowing from unseen TV's, peer from bay windows. They are bathed in broadcast waves, trapped in living rooms, pushing flat against the glass, lapping at the darkness of the unknowable future. We disappear and emerge, into and out of their little galaxies of syndicated goodness, before worm holing back into the sheltering obscurity of the night around us.

Heavy metal screams from the radio, guitars stab at the air, mixing with uncontrolled, teenaged, male laughter. I tear down the street and veer towards a front yard. Cheap beers in hand we bounce over the curb, through a driveway and onto the lawns. Over and over I bounce up and down, one driveway and then another, dirt kicking up from the tires. Finn leans out the passenger side window with a BB gun aimed at the night. CRACK - a front window splinters into a spider web. Beer shoots out of Casper's nose from the backseat.

"Ah shit." Finn drops back into the car, "You see that shit?"

"You guys are fuckin' crazy! Hunter, you've got to take me somewhere." Casper shakes his head at me, not knowing what to do about being caught in the situation. His voice melds with a scared, hesitant laughter and has a way of sounding just like Beavis from MTV when he talks. He sounded that way years before the show came out, and sometimes I swear they must have based the character on him. "I got to get out of here," visions of his overbearing mother are dancing around the back of his brain, tingling his scalp. This is not the sort of action he needs right now. He can feel her shaking head hovering over him.

Finn and I erupt in laughter as I whip the steering wheel 360 degrees. The car spins and slides through a ripe, green lawn, grass spraying onto front porches. I turn back to center, steering expertly through the yards and screaming along with the radio, "cannot kill the family, battery is found in me." Pounding my hand against the dashboard, "Battery . . . BAT - ERRR – EE." The song spins off into the night and we follow it into the shadows. "Thrashing all deceivers, Mashing non-believers, never ending potency." Tire tracks snake away towards the horizon.

Harbor Bay stretches about 3 miles wide, east to west, along Lake Erie's shores. At its tallest point, it reaches south three quarters of a mile to the Norfolk Southern railroad tracks, which serve as the town's southern border. Strict laws against commercialization keep it quaint and filled with locally owned family stores. A coffee shop, pharmacy, a couple of bakeries, auto repair places and a small candy shop fill the various store fronts and brick buildings. It is a privileged town of picket fences and spoiled kids in fast cars and sunglasses. Soccer and baseball fields stretch south from the lake, flanking a playground, a couple of beach volleyball courts, a sled hill and the municipal pool. Watching over all, an audience of fluffy green trees billows up into the air, soft lungs shrouding the hidden creaks and streams which slide through the hills, down to an expansive beach and large mansions on the lake's shores. On summer days, past the bird chirped soccer games, pretty girls strut their wares down the sidewalks in gilded fashion shows. And at night, beyond the outfield walls, out by the darkened swing sets and high dives - orange embers make their way from swing to swing, pinched fingers to pinched fingers. Stories are told, gossip is born and the ball field spotlights mix with distant streetlamps to light the carefree universe - only possible in a town such as this.

Police headquarters doubles as City Hall and sits on a plush piece of land in the center of it all. Right now, fifty yards from there, a couple of pool-hopping kids bob up and down in the water like some drunken, wanna-be Navy Seals. Snickering, they watch the cops cross the parking lot at shift change and jab at each other, trying to make the other laugh as though they were in a library. An officer arriving for the night shift shoots a look over in their direction, sending a bolt of panic through them.

"Shhhh," they calm each other's chuckles. But the officer continues on past, unaware of their existence. It's the pinnacle of 12-year old, pre-pubescent joy to pull off this full-on affront to the police. Soon they'll show up somewhere with wet, matted hair and spin their tale of close calls. Word will spread of their successful mission and their rite of passage will be cemented in history. They watch the cop disappear behind the force's brand spanking new, armored, white Hummer. At first read, it could be just a symptom of overzealous, rent-a-cop inferiority complexes mixed with nosy, over-protective parents and too much tax money. Unfortunately, the symptom has a much more dire prognosis.

Down in the basement, below the Police Station, the Westshore Enforcement Bureau (WEB) is unpacking their new surveillance equipment. Only two of the crew are here now, but they're the major players on the team of six. Dan O'Riley, a special agent with the Cleveland FBI's field office and liaison to the Harbor Bay Police Department, is pulling night vision goggles, ease dropping devices and camouflaged surveillance cameras out of their Styrofoam packing. Pat Ramsey sits in the corner, drinking coffee out of a cup from Harbor Java, the local cafe across the street in The Center. Ramsey is a slight man and - at all of 26 - still looks like a teenager. It's the one obvious reason he was chosen to go into Harbor Bay High School as a "transfer student". He also had three years of solid fieldwork in Gary, Indiana before the request for an in-school agent was sent out.

"It's sophisticated network with meticulous layers they've got going." Ramsey is saying as he unwraps some equipment. "We obviously know Waylon is doing the bulk of it, but there's a dozen others running their own little businesses." Waylon Jones is the local kingpin, a 16-year old kid running a healthy marijuana empire and beginning to dabble in more lucrative product as well. Ramsey has been attempting to get close to him for some months now.

"And we're sure Waylon is not supplying them all?" O'Riley asks.

"He is most of the time, but I think the rest of them have their own connections to keep him out whenever possible and eliminate another cut being taken."

"Bringgggg. Beep. Beep. Beep." Dispatchers funnel 911 calls into the Harbor Bay Police Station now. Normally our turfing antics would not be discovered until the morning, but the BB pellet through the window understandably incites a quicker reaction tonight. Officers spring to life inside the station house. Round here this profession generally draws two types of characters - hard ass,

9

mirrored sunglass wanna-be military types and belly hanging over the belt good old boys. In order to live out their dream, the good old boys train as hard as they can for a few months to pass that initial physical, and then promptly never again do anything about it. Teenagers love outrunning these guys while generally fearing the crew-cut diehards, who come across as so unhinged that any wise-ass teenager can instantly picture himself or herself being beaten to a pulp and then thrown in a cell to boot.

Now theoretically the turf marks should be able to tell the AUTHORITIES all they need to know and allow them to quickly deduce this crime scene to be the work of teenagers; but offenses like this instantly draw 5 alarm bells, especially since the Chief of Police, John Waters, is still milling about the station a couple of hours after normal business hours. Waters is of the good old boy variety and this burst of excitement tickles his loins. He's already picturing the little blurb in the local paper about how he quickly handled this and brought the perpetrators to justice. Plus, you never know - it could be blacks coming over from the east side to terrorize the town - best be on alert. Instead of delegating some actions, he overzealously radios out to a couple of cruisers himself, "Head towards Diversey and set up a 8 block perimeter." He says, giving them the direction a few of the silhouettes said the car appeared to be headed. Next he sends a team of deputies out to the address of the broken window. Other than that, he doesn't have much to go on. Fuck him.

We're already past their rink-a-dink perimeter and I drive over the tracks into Southlake in order to let things cool down and get some food. Cruising down an industrial parkway we fly over the highway and up to the main commercial intersection. It's purposely a different world in the town next door - strip malls lined with khaki pants and cheap jewelry. The entire area is an exponentially expanding mass of brick, glass and neon product, all designed to dazzle the monkey brain. It extends out from the traffic light, where it seems as though each year they add a new lane to accommodate the suburban throngs. There are 12 movie theaters and too many stores filled with cheap clothes, bad posters and trinkets for days. Remnants of the 70's are reflected in the weathered brick of the fast food restaurants that take up the inner most square of the intersection. A McDonald's, Wendy's and Burger King take up three of the four corners.

"Oh here he is again - The fucking fast food bandit." Finn rolls his eyes at me as I pull into the McDonalds.

"That's right fuck nuts." A boy has to eat and on nights like this, I jump out and drop into a little method acting. I got the idea one night when I was working at this same McDonalds and got suspicious of an obese customer claiming that we had shorted him of 2 Quarter Pounders. Judging his pupils skeptically I realized it was a brilliant way to feed myself when broke - not that I'm broke now, but I know every penny I have is going to go to alcohol – that's how it is for me. It's harmless fun as I walk up to the counter and act all disgruntled, pretending that I had to take 30 seconds out of my life because of the drive thru window's incompetency. But I'll forgive it all if they just hand over the Quarter Pounder with Cheese they left out of my order. I drop it through my driver's side window and head across the street. At Wendy's I tell them they forgot my fries and a Vanilla shake from Burger King. All good, I jump back into the car and turn to Finn.

"Don't you fuckin eyeball my shit mother fucker."

"You're lucky I didn't eat it all why you were running around like the freak you are." He talks through a mouthful of fries pushing out from behind his teeth and I grab him by the back of the head as he laughs and chokes.

"Get a room and let's go. Fucking faggots." Casper, anxious to escape us, is all antsy in the backseat.

"I need to go by The Center and see if my brother is there." I say, nonchalantly backing out of the parking lot.

"Bullshit!" Finn calls me on my lie. "Poppy is supposed to be there with Annie. They called me before you picked me up and said you were going to swing by."

"I never said that shit."

"Right." Casper pops his head in between us from the backseat, chiding. "There's no shame in wanting a little dry humping action," a little Beavis snicker follows.

"Get the fuck out of here!" I scoff with a fake backhand. "Dry humping? What you do is your own business, I gave up grinding on legs in 8th grade."

"Shit!" Finn rolls his eyes at me. "You'd grind on a log. Give me a bite of that." He swipes at my Quarter Pounder, I block him and laugh to myself.

"I would fuck a log."

Friday night, football stadium lights shine over the treetops in the distance as we pull into The Center, a mini-mall directly across from the Police Station. The lights of the game cast a haloed glow over the town as though a UFO has landed in a field nearby. The Center is a big square parking lot surrounded by little stores and the unofficial meeting place slash starting point for most Harbor weekend nights. Tonight is no exception. It's a typical, fall, pre-game crowd. Posing skaters roll around the admiring Betty's as junior high football players and cheerleaders pretend like they're next in line to be the star quarterback and homecoming queen. Groups of shiftless hooligans mill about the edges of the buildings, smoking cigarettes and using the shadows to hide their plots and schemes. Secretly they trade Black Flag and D.R.I. cassettes, discuss Minor Threat's seminal album and generally hate everyone, but themselves. A few make clandestine trips to the payphone at the gas station, placing calls to try and score some weed. They stand with shifty eyes, covering their mouths and whispering as though someone can hear them, never knowing, that thanks to various judicial decrees and other circumstances, every payphone in town is tapped and people can indeed hear every unintelligible word they mumble. Still their main goal, and really everyone's main goal, is to figure out how they're going to get beer tonight. It's a life or death proposition with this crowd. No one wants to be wandering the streets with nothing to take their mind from the boredom of it all.

There are only a handful of kids who everyone knows has a good fake ID and our buddy, Hayden, is one of them. He's across the way, at the gas station around the corner, surrounded by dozens of single-pubed freshman. They've been jockeying to be around him since the start of the evening, hoping to have one of the 12-packs rolling out of the store in the shopping cart be theirs. Like a seller at the stock exchange, he takes orders, looks at bills and calculates the change they'll never get back. He throws a chastising look at pimply kid trying to pay him too little, keeping his arm extended until the bills makes sense for all involved. The hopeful quickly learn to overpay and curry favor for never ending weekends to come. Hayden hasn't had to pay for a single night out since his look-alike brother in college turned 21 and hooked him up.

But he can only buy so much beer and out on the fringes, hapless stragglers access their fate. The realization that they will not be a part of tonight's lottery sets in, dejected heads pout downward, the specter of a sober night crystalizes in the dark air around them. They turn bad fake ID's over in their hands, knowing them to be worthless. False promises of hope and teenage oblivion dissipate into forlorn parent's basements and lonely video games. Only the desperate will disperse into their death throes and spread out to the 3 different convenient stores around town, leaning against the old brick of store walls, eyes casting about, hoping to spot a 'cool' looking adult who will buy the beer for them. The courage to ask the right one rarely ever comes.

Acting nonchalant as I find a parking spot, my eyes dart about longingly for the sight of Poppy. Finn jumps out of the car first, all hopped up and giggling. "He's a handsome little devil," as my mom liked to say. Everyone loves him, not only for his good looks, but also because his mischievousness humor emanates from a truly good soul. A bouncing leprechaun of a human, his continually upturned lips are contagious as he needles and devises ways to make everyone around him happy. Even if you've never met him before, he'll walk into your house as though he'd been there a million times, really believed your castle was his castle, and in an instant you loved him for opening up your cupboards without asking. He is already walking through the crowd, high fiving everyone is sight. Casper slips off to the side and heads over to some skaters and borrows a board. I get the distinct feeling he's had enough of us for the night.

Thinking I've missed Poppy, my heart is sinking by the nanosecond. But just as I'm about to fall into the abyss I see the blur of her darkly angelic figure materialize from the drugstore, an otherworldly apparition promising things unconfined by this place. My spirits rise as I step out of the car, the weight of her magnetic force lifting me up. The night sky has buoyancy to it. The fall air is brisk on my skin and feels vibrant and visceral on my eyeballs. I stretch my arms out and take it all in. Feeling alive I let out a little half yell, half grunt as though I'm some silverback surveying the land and staking out my territory. I watch impressed as Casper does a legit heel flip over one of the benches that line the sidewalk of the shops and hands the board back to a couple of awestruck kids. They will spend the rest of the night trying to emulate him, cracking into benches and sending their boards hurling in all directions. This will inevitably draw the wrath of the shop owners and then the police, who hate nothing more than these little punks with their weird hair and clothes, whom they'll never understand. Finn has already made it over to Poppy and Annie and has them laughing hysterically. I start my b-line towards them thinking if he's talking shit on me, I'll jump the little fucker right here.

Poppy recently moved here from somewhere in California and from that first moment I first saw her, I missed her. I have spent every moment since that appearance wondering where she is and filled with a deep, gut wrenching pain because of it. A need to be swallowed by her being has consumed me. The mysterious vortex of darkness swirling about her, a magnet I don't have the capacity to yet realize is existential awareness, pulls me in. Her dark hair and features frame beautiful blue-white wolf like eyes and are filled with infinite questions. There's more weight to her pupils than anyone I have ever known and her presence has made irrelevant the existence of all the little Nike wearing, day-glow cuties prancing about. She has an expansive illegality about her that chides my own intrinsic, adventurous nature. Only by being around her do I understand for the first time the use of the word *heavy*. She has something no one else in this town has, and I want.

"Hey," I say to all three of them, sheepishly catching Poppy's eyes. Finn and Annie allow her to answer.

"How are you?" She says.

"I'm feeling good." I say emphatically with a big smile. Then that's it. That's all I got. I'm the worst at this small talk shit. Jesus fuck! I want to say, I really like you, I have a back seat. We can go fog up the windows behind the Holiday Inn. I'm a sixteen-year old idiot. But I like her and I hope she likes me. Deep. Idiot. Jesus fuck! She just looks through me until Finn steps in to save me from pissing on myself like the invalid I am.

"We just tore some shit up over by Casper's house. It was fun as fuck." As he says this, I turn towards my car and look at the mud covering the back of it. Just then - headlights shine across the thick lines of dirt sprayed out from the wheel wells, highlighting the indisputable evidence clinging to the backside of the car. Temporarily blinded, our eyes follow the beams of light to the cop car bouncing up the slight incline into The Center.

"Shit!" Finn and I say simultaneously. Even for these halfwits, it won't take much to put two and two together. Thinking the same thing, we grab the girls and walk brusquely towards the rear of my car. I yell out, "CASPER!" Waving him over with my voice sending a clear message, *get over here now!*

Leading the girls by the hand, we reform our little circle around the rear bumper as Casper jogs over.

"What's up?" He starts to say and then sees the cruiser approaching.

"Stand here." He understands in an instant, and although he's worried about being incriminated, we reach critical mass just in time and mask the dirt marks as they pass. Inside the patrol car are two notorious, hard ass officers looking menacing. We realize that due to our earlier antics, the cavalry is out tonight - even more than usual. They glare at us, but their lizard brains are now more concerned with the kids in the skater garb, whom they'd give their left nut to be able to crack right in the face and teach them a real lesson about obeying "No Skateboarding" signs. The skaters see them too late. In no time at all they are pressed against the hood of the cruiser and handcuffed, the whole scene creating an escape diversion for us. I become aware of Poppy's hand in mine. I turn to her - electrified, justified, full. Something has sparked within her. I see a new look of intrigue inside the white light of her eye. Squeezing her hand, I let the sexual tension build and bubble out into the air around her until we can barely take it.

"What are you doing after the game?" I ask her, my teenage hard on pressing painfully against my belt.

"I don't know yet. I can't be out that late."

"You want me to give you a ride home or something?"

"Sure. Thanks." Her smile crushes and lifts me simultaneously. I collapse inwards, 80,000 babies left in the pre-cum on my jeans.

"Ok." I say to her as Finn and I share a knowing look, "We've got some things to do." As we move to get back in my car, I look around for Casper and catch him, head down, taking a drag off a joint in the corner. "Casper, you coming with us?"

He looks up and waves me off, "Nah, you go ahead."

"Cool." I respond and turn back to Poppy. "I'll find you at the game." She casts a predatory nod that sends my teenage hormones into a tizzy. I try to take to shake off the overwhelming longing and jump in the car, but the thought is pervasive and all I can think about is finding her later. I growl and Finn laughs knowingly.

We spin away from the bright lights of The Center and head towards Waylon's house. We need to get to a hose quick, destroy the evidence and get the BB gun out of our car ASAP before diving headlong into what this Friday night holds. Besides the fact that Finn has some business to take care of with Waylon, his house also offers a sanctuary no one else's does. Even if his dad, Tripp, is home, he won't hassle us with questions about what we've been doing.

Tripp is a frontiersman, an innovator, a seer. In the early years of online multi-player role-playing games, he had become fascinated with the lengths people would go to in order to earn virtual weapons and strength for their internet avatars. These people lived an entirely separate existence within these games and there were no laws to the vaguely understood worldwide web. Tripp took advantage. In order to purchase items and secret powers in game, players need to earn gold or some other virtual currency. But this currency was all imaginary, created by the people who made the games. In short, software, written in 0's and 1's by a human. Tripp figured he could just re-code the currency and open up his own black market, selling the currency at greatly reduced prices. No more having to stay up 3 days straight and lose your job to get some glowing semen to defeat that dragon, come to Tripp's website and purchase your own for fantasy land domination.

It would be years before the internet laws caught up to this sort of pirating, but for now business was thriving and Tripp was able to pay a bunch of us good money, whenever we wanted, to go troll around inside these games and chat people up – virtually. We let them know about an easy way to get that super power they so desperately needed. When we first started all we did was talk up the female players with cute avatars, so Tripp wised up and starting paying us commission. We quickly learned to turn ourselves into cute avatars and go after the overly fantasized, male, online personas that were all more than eager to talk to us. That's where the money is.

To avoid the cops slowly stalking about, I weave through side streets as much as possible, but the drive is crosstown and we have to pop out into the open eventually to make it there. As we pull up to a red light next to the middle school, we see two cop cars approaching. Panic envelops from all directions as we lower our beer cans. They're a quarter mile a way and it feels like a high noon showdown. I'm frozen at the stop for too long. We watch as time devolves from slow motion to a standstill. Their lights flick on and the burst of the siren drops our hearts into our stomachs. Our heads turn to follow them as they jettison past us. "Somebody's toilet papering someone." Finn chuckles nervously. We exhale and silently make our way towards Waylon's house, nervously sipping our beers.

The ever-present computer glow shines from Tripp's study as I whip all the way round to the back of his house. The quaint exterior masks the complexity of the worlds inside where virtual and real world currencies are being made in sorted ways. I know where the spigot is and go to the hose as Waylon comes strutting outside with a massive, blissed out smile. He's a ditz normally and now that he's been pulling on balloons for a couple of hours, he's trying to keep his head from drifting up towards the sky. His baby blue eyes roll towards the back of his head as he telepathically invites you to join the cloud he's on. Sun-In products bolster his naturally, dirty, blond hair - his ever-present tan and jewelry hint at a streak of Guido. However, the town's faux preppy influence grounds him slightly. It shows through as his hemp bracelets and beads mingle with his flashy jewelry. This alone separates him from the silk shirt wearing types downtown. Still, with his puffed up, Nautilus trained body; he oozes cheese in an already plastic town. We love him for all of these traits, because of his awareness of them and the pleasure he takes in the image he creates of himself. And more to HIS point, there's a certain class of girl that loves him for this persona, as much as his endless supply of kind bud.

We pull the rest of the 12 pack out from the hatchback, crack some and start spinning Waylon tales of a bad ass drift I pulled off across a two yard stretch and the window cracking in symmetric beauty. As we reminisce, he let's out little gasps of air, "Heh . . . Heh," his laugh a mirror into his fried brain. You can hear the neurons trying to connect - this gets us all going and our laughter fills the air with all the fucking blind innocence of youth. The world is light and no amount of THC paranoia even comes close to alerting us to the reality of the moment - We are being watched. A state of the art camera made to look like a small nob of bark, essentially invisible to the human eye, sits high in a backyard tree snapping photos of us all. Like feds at a Mafioso funeral, every car in Waylon's driveway has their license plate recorded. Only years later in a Cuyahoga County courtroom would I see the frozen images of this night – SNAP - my head thrown back in laughter, mouth open, howling at the sky – SNAP - chasing Finn into the house with hose - Ones for the scrapbook, or exhibit A - depending on who's looking.

I'm chasing Finn around the garage when he ducks behind a corner and tries to ambush me. He hits me with a double leg, but I recover by aiming the hose into his face and drench him fucking good as I go down.

"All right, All right, shit." He stands in wide-eyed disbelief that I'd actually soak him. "I have to go home and change now." He says disgusted, snapping his arms and shaking the water from off of him.

"Oh you'll be fine." Waylon has snapped back into reality, "Go grab something out of my room." Finn gives me the stink eye as he walks away, letting me know he's plotting revenge. Grudgingly he goes inside, all his care in picking the perfect outfit for the night for naught. We follow him in since they want a couple hits from the bong before heading over to the game.

Downstairs we climb into the crawlspace that serves as the modern day, teen equivalent of an opium den. It's covered in tapestries and band posters. Black lights and strings of Christmas lights fill it's universe. Sitting against the wall, knowing I'll be able to drive fine, I'm content with my beer buzz and don't partake. I watch them cough out the plumes of smoke and soak in the lyrics of The Doors, "Can you picture what will be, so limitless and free." It might as well be 1968 in here as I try to take in the full meaning of it all, never knowing that three blocks away our lives are changing forever.

Snitch

A spotlight shines through the back window of an old, two-tone brown and tan Monte Carlo. Red and blue lights reflect off the front windows of houses and broadcast their presence up into the trees. The thick dust on the car's back window glows like stretched cotton and casts specks of shadows throughout the interior of the car, making it seem as though cobwebs and particles hang from the rays of red, white and blue light. "Oh shit, shit." Tom Nelson says to himself as he crams a couple of bags of cocaine into the cracks of his seat and stares feverishly into the rearview mirror. Despite his hard ass reputation, he's got some serious product on him and is scared shitless. Two officers approach from either side of the car and he's shaking, desperately telling himself to calm down.

"Mr. Nelson, place your hands out the driver side window please." His car is known in this town – as is every other potential troublemaker's. The earlier vandalism combined with his reputation is cause enough to stop him and see what he's been up to this evening, an easy target. The officer on the passenger side is scanning around the car and when he looks into the back seat, sees a clear dime bag filled with cocaine has slid through the seat and onto the back floor mat. He raises his head above the car roof, motions to his partner and uses his flashlight to spotlight the package for him.

Despite coming from a good home, Tom Nelson, known to everyone, his age, just as Nelson – with a deep foreboding weight to it - has an edge to that belies this town. Something Casper, Finn and I had always noticed. Even back in grade school we were always aware of it lurking. It was palpable, simultaneously intriguing and frightening. It felt at is if he could blow something up at any second or become unhinged and lunge at whoever was around. The sharpness that came through in his snide remarks for every teacher was beyond typical smart-ass disdain. He always pushed the envelope, took things too far, too cruel. He wore down the patience of anyone in a position of authority. He was into harder things, drawn to the wrong side of the tracks, always had been. Still, we liked him for innumerable reasons and watched from the sidelines as he ventured further out onto the edge into a world that was foreign to us.

Along with a growing criminal reputation he was also gaining some notoriety as a flyweight boxer with quick hands and no quit. Even before he began boxing he was known as an incredibly tenacious scrapper, willing to throw down with anyone, even older kids twice his size. In a failed attempt to give him some direction his father had signed him up with a trainer at a well-known gym downtown. Nelson spent a lot of time there and now that he was actually training, his muscle fibers pressed against his thin skin, striating like rubber bands around his bones. His hands were becoming increasingly fast, blurring like the wings of a hummingbird, as he'd hit the bag. At the gym they were prepping him for a pro career, but he was only vaguely interested in that. He was however interested in the allure of the street life that a lot of the kids in the gym brought with them. Over the last couple of years he had spent a little time in juvie, further deepening his exposure to elements that we in our coddled states had yet to conceive existed outside of the movies. He was the only person in our school who had a tattoo, a large circle on his chest that housed boxing gloves in the shape of a yin-yang symbol. He was mixed up with some characters and it was all incredibly seedy to us, real and unreal, we wanted to know more.

"I'm going to need you to step out of the car."

Watching from the back seat of the cruiser as they tear apart his car, he knows this is beyond parents being pissed, beyond juvie. Two other patrol cars pull up behind him. He starts sweating.

The game is in full swing as the crowds taunt each other across the field - venomous chants echoing out in the chilled fogged air like cold fronts colliding. "Your town sucks, no your town sucks." Word has spread that some senior is looking to beat up my little brother. The dude is a notorious bully, slash tough guy, who is known to be a martial artist of some sort. I've discovered two things about these types of situations. One – the tough guy's myth is usually just that and Two – strike first. Tracking this kid down is my first order of business and I spot him in the grassy area behind the end zone. The initial adrenaline rush momentarily freezes my body like only cold water or fear can do. I push past it, use it and head over to him. It's as though these parts of stadiums are laid out specifically for high school fight scenes like this. Mr. Jiu-jitsu mother fucker sees me at the last second.

"I hear you're looking for my brother?" I act mellow about it, although I'm charged with energy and invading his space. He looks me up and down, knows a bit about me, but has no choice in the matter. He's been slighted and his hunt for my brother is protocol at this point - as is my response.

"Yeah. What's it to you?" Out of the side of his face, he gives a sly smile to a friend he has next to him. I know the kid, take a quick look in his eyes and am confident he's not going to jump in. "I'm gonna pound his ass as soon as I see him. You gonna do something about it?"

Deep down we both know either one of us could come out on top or end up beaten. STRIKE FIRST. In an instant I block his ankle with my foot, grab him by the throat, throw him off balance and whip him to the ground, pressing his head up against a chain link fence. 12 years of wrestling against the best kids in the country enable me to put the fear of god into any non-wrestler pretty quickly – usually. This time it works and I see the panic in his face. He wiggles against my grip in an attempt to put some half-ass submission hold on me, but he's no match for the grip I've used to hold people down with for years. He can feel my strength against his neck and knows he's in trouble tonight. I'm afraid of him escaping and squeeze harder. A finger on a pressure point lets him know I can do some serious damage if I want. News of the scrap is already making its way past the cotton candied concession booths, turning into a collective excitement that winds through all the gooey, cheese covered nachos and oversized, watery sodas. Any happening in this town is an event of the moment and a possible brawl is big news. Quickly it spreads across the pom-pom laced aluminum stands, finding it's way to my brothers. His skin becomes redder each second and a large vein rises from his temple as I press harder.

"Try a little karate chop now mother fucker! I'll put you in the fuckin' hospital!" I say in a growled low voice, my arms coiled, flexed and primed. He's deciding what to do and so I raise my other hand high as though I'm gonna bury my fist in his temple and end this right now. The possibility is enough.

"All right, all right." He chokes out just as my two brothers run up behind me. My pre-emptive attack the deciding factor.

"Sorry, I just wanted to talk to him." He coughs sheepishly as I let him up. I'm relieved for his apology and experience a slight adrenaline dump.

"What the fuck?" My brother Raleigh walks up and pushes Karate's man's friend with a powerful shove. "You wanna go?"

"No. No Raleigh, we're all good." I grab my brother gently. They're both amped and want to throw fists now. I only fought out of a big brother obligation, but Raleigh, my middle brother, 10 months younger than me, lives for this shit. He has 4 inches and 40lbs on me. He grinds his teeth while looking at me with his crazy eyes, grumbling as he speaks out of the side of his mouth.

"Fuckin "A" Hunter. Let me wail him." Raleigh's a beast and I'm the only one in town who ever gets the better of him. He's a no-holds barred motherfucker when it comes to fighting, and has thrown everything he has at me as well. Even now I have a broken bone in my hand – a boxer's fracture - from just a few weeks ago.

There were a bunch of friends and family over for his 16th birthday party. We're outside playing basketball when Raleigh got pissed about some imaginary slight, thinking I was cheating by being better than him. So he grabs a rake out of the yard and swings it at my head. I block it with my hand - FRACTURE - and then grab it from him in one fluid motion, swing it up into the air, to bring down on his head. He turtles into a ball on the ground and out of mercy; I drop the rake and walk away. After he realizes I had turned, he runs at me and jumps on my back. I throw him off, grab him by the back of his hair and am already throwing his head downwards as I see my grandparents come walking up the

30

driveway - They are a lovely pair of deaf mutes, in their 70's, who came over on the boat from Ireland together. We called them grandma and grandpa "Ewww" because that was the only sound my grandmother could actually hear - I can't stop the inertia and bounce his face off my knee. My eyes lock with theirs as I lift his face back up, his nose exploding, blood flying in all directions. The look of horror on their faces telling me I'm never going to be able to explain what had led to that moment. I let him go and he ran sobbing into the house, blood pouring out between his fingers. Little fucker. Just a month before that he had grabbed a log poker from the fireplace and swung it overhand at my head. I dodged left and the metal hook buried into the back of my shoulder. Filled with rage, I threw him onto the couch with such ease it was surprising to myself and proceeded to punch him in the kidneys until I was convinced he'd be pissing blood – he did for days. The only explanation for me coming out on top in these tassels is some innate understanding in our blood that gives me big brother powers. It drives him mad and causes him to always have a slight undercurrent of wanting to prove he can beat my ass and anyone else's.

"We were just messing around." I say this to allow my new friend to save some face and give him a knowing smile that says *this is done.* His understanding look satisfies my concern and I know that I won't have to go through this with him again. On the other hand, my reassurance to my brothers that it's "all cool" does little to assuage them as they telepathically call me a pussy.

"Come on Hunter, let him go." Rory, the youngest, is small for his age, but has a habit of attracting other guy's girlfriends – thus our current situation. A cute cheerleader is his ulterior motive for chiding me to let Raleigh brawl. I smile at him, letting him I know what he's thinking about. He smiles back nodding, knowing that this guy getting a beat down will only cement his case with said lady, whomever she is.

"Fuck that." I say, "We'll all just end up getting busted." The crowd around us is starting to draw the attention of the rent-a-cops. I turn to the dude. "We're cool right?" He nods, speechless. I'm amazed at how stupid he could be to not realize there'd be three of us to contend with. Senior or not, you don't want to mess with three, two-fisted, too Irish brothers. I nod at him to go and give Raleigh a rub on the shoulders.

"It's all cool, Raleigh, let's get a beer."

He utters a low growl.

"He would have beat your ass anyway." Rory antagonizes Raleigh as we turn to walk away, quite a threesome strolling across the green lawn smattered with students. Raleigh, filled with pent up hostility, shoves Rory a little too hard on the shoulders and sends him stumbling five steps forward.

"Fuckin' Dick!" Rory looks genuinely hurt - sensitive little guy. With less than 3 years separating all of us, we're the best of friends and although we try to contain our testosterone driven energy to outsiders, inevitably we honed our fighting skills on each other growing up. For years to come, random people will come up to our poor mother and say, "I don't know how you did it."

People are staring as we head back through the crowd, proud. I see Poppy with a small group of girls up a grassy little hill. Finn is there also; I'm sure acting as color commentator on my behalf. With his spin, she's seen this play out and although she's not into the normal jock nonsense, suspects there's more to me than that, knows the dynamics of my family and plus, like everybody else, has heard this guy was looking for my little brother. It can all be very impressive to a juvenile brain. I pat my brothers on the back and head over to her. Being the zeitgeist of the moment, she gains some status by my approach - it doesn't take much around here, the importance of high school everything so exaggerated. The referee is whistling for halftime. The people in the stands rise, applauding, as the players do a sideways run past the clapping crowd. They exit the field and leave the Docker wearing, sweater over the shoulder mass in a frenzy.

"Hey, I've been looking for you." I smile at Poppy and she smiles back with glassy eyes. I look closer and see that they're red as well.

"You sure are a tough guy huh?" She giggles, only half mocking.

"I'm something. I don't know what, but I'm something." With a knowing nod, I pull some Visine from my pocket to hand to her. "You guys want to get out of here?"

"Hell yeah!" Finn declares and grabs Annie's giggling hand. I grab Poppy's hand and head out of the stadium, past the cheerleaders ra-ra-ra-ing for scarfed moms and overzealous dads, glad to be gone.

Dirty, black, Converse high tops shuffle slowly on an old linoleum floor through a glossy cement hallway. With red eyes, as though he's been crying, Nelson is let into a drab holding cell inside police headquarters. He takes a couple more hesitant steps into the room and an officer takes off his handcuffs.

"We'll be with you soon."

The door locks ominously as Nelson watches the officer disappear through a small rectangular window in the door. The window is reinforced with diamond shaped wire frames, between glass panes, to make them shatterproof. A surveillance camera in the upper corner of the room stares down at him. In the distance are the sounds of thick doors closing. His hands are stained from the fingerprinting machine. Sitting down, he puts his head on the table in a state of shock - distant and isolated, knowing he's really screwed up this time.

The Chief of Police, John Waters, shoves a handful of chips into his mouth as he watches Nelson's holding cell on a flat screen TV. The security camera footage is crisp on a state of the art system. Detective Jim Spain looks over at the bag of chips and reaches in. He's balding and unkempt. His stomach presses against a stained, cheap linen button down, and bulges grotesquely over his belt. Spittle and crumbs bounce from his lips as he takes a sip of orange soda from a plastic bottle. The pair are feeling justified. They are staring at opportunity.

Operating on vague hunches gleamed from one too many misdemeanor cases; it was these two who had put the call out to the Feds. The informant, Ramsey, had been inside the High School for eight months now and was coming up empty. All these seedy stakeouts, schemes, Hummers and night vision goggles were amounting to file cabinets of nothing and they were feeling the heat of their budget requests and bold proclamations about the prolific drug trade going on in our little town. Now with some real drugs, and the assumption of Nelson's shady connections, they were primed with anticipation.

"We've got something here." At 46, Spain is five years Chief Waters' junior, and only harbors mild ambitions of taking over that role. From the looks of him however, diabetes or a heart attack will get him first.

"I agree." Chief Waters nods, "We need to turn this kid."

"His dad will end up helping us when he gets here."

"You think so?"

"He's no dummy. Something like this could ruin him." Spain pauses to check himself, "Yeah, they'll turn."

"Why don't you go warm him up to the idea. Let him know he's really stepped in it tonight. I'll go talk to Agent O'Riley." Waters says, heading off downstairs with the good news.

Nelson hears the door open and looks up as Detective Spain enters the room holding a small Dixie cup and a piece of paper. He gives Nelson a look of sympathy and speaks softly.

"This is a tough spot you've gotten yourself into Tom." He slides a chair over to the table and places the Dixie cup on the table. It has orange soda in it and few floating chip crumbs.

"Your dad should be here in a little bit. I've got some people I'm going to need you talk to. I think you're going to learn a bunch of things tonight that will blow your mind." Spain slides a piece of paper over to him and pulls a pen out of his shirt pocket.

"I'm going to need you to read and sign this piece of paper, which informs you of your constitutional rights." Spain shrugs his shoulders casually as Nelson looks up at him doe-eyed.

"Go on, read it."

Nelson scans the paper as Spain speaks nonchalantly to brush over the seriousness of his signature.

"Generally what it means is that you don't have to make any statement, and any statement you make can be used against you. You can get a lawyer if you want, etc." He gives one more nod to Nelson, who then signs the paper.

"All right good. I'm going to step outside and wait for your father. I need to have a little talk with him."

The thought of his dad sends a shudder through him. He's put his father through some tests before and although some of his antics may seem extreme in the soft bubble of Harbor Bay, in reality they were fairly tame in the scope of things. Heavy with the breath of an obese man, Spain pushes his fat arm onto the table to lift himself. He grabs the Dixie cup and with that he exits the room, now vast and empty. Nelson sits in silence, stares off, shakes his head and mumbles to himself in disbelief.

The little red 450SL convertible pops up a small incline and pulls into the Station's parking lot. Robert Nelson – Bob – throws his car into park and exits shaking his head. *How many times is he going to have to come down here to this damn station and bail his son out?* He's a svelte man who has for years worked to rise about his blue-collar upbringing. Only his slightly weathered features hint at his past as his socialite ambitions and pretentions envelope him a country club veneer. Familiar enough with the place to know his way around, he walks through the small garage and into a side door, emerging into a little hallway inside. He's on a mission as he rounds a corner and approaches the front desk. The quicker he facilitates this release, the less time he'll have to endure the stares of these goddamn public servants who have no idea what it takes to build the mini-empire he's built. Hell, he's a famous architect in some circles – namely a 30-mile radius from where he now stands. Maybe expand that circle some with all the notoriety from his messy divorce that the piss ant locals papers loved to splash around in black and white. *Whatever, fuck all those Know-Nothings, I'll just barrel through them all.*

"I'm here to post bond for Tom Nelson." He's all business.

The officer on duty looks up from his Sports Illustrated with a barely constrained smirk. It's gonna take a little more than your money tonight he thinks to himself. "Hold on a moment." He heads off slowly down the hall.

Agent O'Riley is in Water's office talking to the Chief. Detective Spain stands in the corner of the room, arms folded.

Waters is saying, "I just don't think they're ever going to trust Agent Ramsey to be one of them. You know how these cliques are."

"I disagree. I've seen this a dozen times and it takes a while to survey the situation, get past the new guy syndrome and start making some headway. If we try to turn this kid into a C.I. then we're putting him in some serious danger. You don't know whom we're dealing with yet. Sure he's got a bit of a rap sheet, but its all minor things. He comes from a good family. I don't feel good about setting him down this path. I say we flip him, get his connection and go from there."

"No. This is my arrest. I obviously want your blessing as I think this will be a great asset to the both of us, but I know this kid, I know his family. It's our perfect storm. He's already in with all the players and his dad will force him to play ball." He pauses for a moment and lets the truth come out. "I need this. I want this."

The officer from the front desk knocks on the open door frame.

"Excuse me Chief, Mr. Nelson is here."

"Thanks." He stands up and says to O'Riley, "I'll bring him in here and lay it out for him. I'd love your help. You can feel it out and put a stop to it whenever you want. If you're really against it, I'll listen to you."

"It's your jail." O'Riley says, appreciating the quick, rational concession.

Bob Nelson circles the lobby head down, hand on his chin, thinking when

Chief Waters appears, portraying a mood of empathy, "Bob, sorry to see you under these circumstances."

"Yeah. Tell me about it. What's his bond this time?" He doesn't even ask what he did, assuming it's another open container or misdemeanor pot charge or some other such non factor.

Waters shakes head and lets out a long exhale to let Bob know this is a doozy. "Judge is saying 100k."

"100k, what the fuck? Did he kill somebody?" All that he needs now is more bad press. A goddamn sentence in the Police Blotter alone could kill the Public Square Development project at this point. If his son costs him a 26 million dollar project . . .

"Why don't you come on back to my office and talk for a moment?"

Bob Nelson looks around, drops his head and follows Waters down the hallway.

Detective Spain has a grim look on his face as they enter. "Bob." He nods.

"Hi Jim." Bob Nelson turns to look at the curly-haired Irish man in front of him and then to Chief Waters as if waiting for an introduction.

"Bob, this is Agent Dan O'Riley with the FBI."

Bob Nelson's mouth drops at the corners, realizing the night is getting considerably longer, and much more dark.

"Mr. Nelson, good to meet you."

They shake hands and both take a seat across from Waters. Detective Spain walks out of the room and returns second later with a folding chair. In an instant Bob Nelson is surrounded by some serious looking officers.

They lay out the details of the arrest for him and their plan to ask Tom to become a Confidential Informant inside the school. A narc. A snitch. It's either that or he's looking at some serious jail time and something on his record that will never go away. There's a serious problem in the community they say. They don't know where it's coming from or how high it goes. They'll need Tom to make cases, make purchases, record conversations and report on happenings. There is no mention of Agent Ramsey. They watch as a hard man, who has dealt with the toughest the construction trade has to offer, withers before their eyes. When it boils down to it, for all his talk of tough love, it's really just love for the baby boy he always wanted. He wipes tears from his eyes occasionally. He thinks about calling the boy's mother, but decides against it. It's his decision and he'll tell his boy to do it. He'll have protection they assure him. It will allow them time to plan a move to a new life somewhere else a year or two down the road.

"Listen. Nobody else knows the two of you are here."

Cold air seeps through the cement walls and directly into Tom's bones. He pulls his knees up to his chest and gives a little shudder. *Has it been 30, 60 minutes?* His buzz is coming down hard now and the jonesing for more powder is electrifying the back of his head and neck. The hair on his forearms stands up and the need feeds a growing anger at his captors, but it will eventually turn him into a defenseless child. The door clicks opens and he turns his head to see Chief Waters and then another man he's never seen. The unknown man sets off his radar.

"Tom, this is Special Agent O'Riley, . . . he's with the FBI."

A reality shift runs across Tom's face as his eyes roll to the back of his head in a wave of disbelief. He gulps and holds back the nausea. Waters lets it hang in the air for the realization to sink in. It's a calculated risk, a pre-emptive attack at Tom's psyche. They are betting he will play along because the last thing they need is for him to be locked up, or out on bail and blabbing about the FBI talking to him. The authorities are all in, in a poker game he doesn't yet know he's entered.

"How do you do Tom?" O'Riley takes a seat methodically. "Just so you know. This is not going to be a little good cop, bad cop routine. We're both bad cops. You're in more trouble than you know right now. I know you're a smart kid. We're going to make you an offer. I want you to listen. I'm going to lay out two paths before you right now. Both of them are going to seem unreal to you, but trust me, both are a reality. One allows you to do the right thing, the other leads to a whole lot of pain." He shrugs his shoulders very matter of fact. "Some people prefer pain. The world is full of dumb people who are optimistic that everything will turn out right in the end no matter what. Let me tell you Tom - that is not the case. Life can be bad, very, very bad. Things don't always turn out right. Tonight we're going to find out how smart you are."

Chief Waters looks on, listening intently. He was not expecting more than a few words from O'Riley, but he's momentarily mesmerized and has to snap himself out of it. The stage is set for him. "We want you to come work for us Tom. I've vouched for you with the F.B.I.," they're long time friends now, "told them you were a smart kid from a good family."

Tom's eyes grow wider by the second. The last remnants of the coca plant play tricks on his brain, spiking his neurons with the final grandiose delusions of invincibility. This is an affront to his character. These fucking cops are questioning his very existence, doubting everything he is.

"You want me to be a snitch?" His mouth hangs open as his eyes dart back and forth between them. Their silence confirms the situation "Fuck that. No way in hell man. No fucking way." He pushes back in his seat like that's the end of it. Spain leans back in his chair and exhales loudly, while Tom searches him for a reaction, the other path.

Agent O'Riley is calm. "I don't give a shit if you do it. Truth is I'd rather see you get put away. For some reason Chief Waters here wants to spare you that future. Like I said, there are two options before you. They are real. Maybe you are dumb and you don't think a few years in the federal pen will be that bad. You can handle it, you think. Boxing a guy in a ring is not the same as fighting off a half dozen guys in the shower. I've looked kids your age in the eye after one week there and it's terrifying – rips my soul out. You'll be broken, used and destroyed by animals. You will *never* be the same. You think you're a tough guy. You're not. I'm not being a dick. I'm just telling you. You are nothing."

"I'm only 17."

"Doesn't matter. You'll stay in juvie 4 months until you're 18 and then be transferred. Most likely you'll be locked up until you're 21."

Every paranoid delusion becoming reality - the scene again becomes slightly surreal through Tom's eyes, Slinking down into his chair, he drops his head back and stares up at the ceiling. Spain leans back with a satisfied smile.

"Your dad's outside. I'm going to bring him in here to talk about this with you. He's in agreement that this is the way to go."

The vast universe inside Tom's young head is being inundated with streams of dialogue flowing in from space. He's having hard time keeping his skull together as its flooded with a million imagined conversations and scenarios, assumed responses and the destruction of the façade he's created for himself over the years. The carefully cultivated hard ass is becoming a . . . ? *No. This cannot be happening.* Broken, he finishes the slouch, his arms dropping to his side as his brain sizzles like pop rocks in child's mouth.

18 months later

I'm sitting on a trainer's table in the locker room. A nurse squirts some cold gel onto my knee and begins rubbing an ultrasound wand all around it. It feels amazing and even though I probably don't need the therapy any longer, I tell everyone my knee hurts just for this feeling. I've just had my body fat measured and it's at just over 4%. Three months ago they had taken a few of us over to the Cleveland Clinic and had us submerged in some pool of water to find out our muscle density and determine what the minimum weight we could possibly get down to was. I'm maxed out, but the coaches are convinced I can win the state championship at this weight. I'm so tired and weak I just don't feel the same as they do. I've lost 30lbs and with my cheeks and eyes sunken in I look like a skeleton of a concentration camp ghost. Anything I've eaten in the last 3 days has come back out in the shower after sticking my fingers down my throat. Even though it was 30 degrees out last night, I slept in the nude and "drifted" 3 lbs. - a process which forces the body to work extraordinarily hard to stay warm and burn calories. We just finished a masochistic 2-hour morning practice in a 105 degree room, the morning before an afternoon match, and I still have a pound to lose in the next 3 hours. I'm in a daze, my head tingling and light. All that I can think of is a drink of water after weigh-ins. As soon as I have a few sips I'll put 15lbs back on instantly as my cells re-hydrate. By the time of my match I could be 25lbs overweight. Yes this will give me a size advantage over my opponents, but there's always a chance my body won't recover.

The nurse finishes my knee and I push up from the table to go take a shower. Tempering the dizziness, right now I'm just concerned with keeping myself from opening my mouth and gulping down the shower water, blowing all my work and missing weight - I've done it before. I'll let it hit my lips and tease the thirst by slowly start suctioning drops into my mouth. Once you start drinking there is no stopping, eventually the body's cravings become overwhelmingly automated. I'll open the bottom of my mouth like a pelican and just let it pour in. If I can't control myself I'll be forced to spend the rest of the afternoon running mile after mile, in plastics, to try and get back down. Today the thought of that future pain keeps me from breaking.

The sun comes through a high window spreading throughout the large shower in a buttery glow. Steam floats up into the gold, clinging on the slippery floors and walls. I lean against the bricks and just let the warm water be all my comfort in the world. My lips are dry and cracking and I'm nothing but bone, skin and muscle. I'm fading, trying to remember that nothing lasts, as Finn comes around the corner ghost-like. He's in the same situation, one weight class above me.

"Gonna get fucked up tonight." His voice is flat and serious.

"Yeah. No shit."

He hangs his towel over the handles of an empty shower spot and places his bottle of medical grade iodine on the soap tray. We all shower with it to fight off staph infections and impetigo. "I got a special treat for us tonight." He's chiding me. Finn loves his weed and is always on my case because I stick to alcohol. He's the team captain and guaranteed to win states. Everyone and their mothers would shit themselves if they knew how much he smoked.

"How much more you got to lose?" I ask.

"I'm good. I'm there. I'm just gonna go to sleep for a bit when I get home. What about you? You look like shit."

"Another pound. I should be good. I'll cut off my pinkies or something." I start thinking of my pill and the secret that I don't even tell Finn about. A friend of ours is a hyperactive kid and he's been on Ritalin for his entire adolescence. One day he was telling me about how it was actually speed, but because of his condition it had a counter effect and helped him to concentrate. I asked him what it was like and he told me it made him feel amazing and he was hardly ever hungry. I was like "DING. DING. DING." *The doctor gives you something that makes you feel amazing, that must be OK then.* I'd been using for the last 3 weeks to try and make it through the end of the season. It definitely helped with the appetite suppression and it was also definitely contributing to the tingling going on in my head. We finish up and towel off on the old, wooden benches tilting between dented, aluminum lockers. I reach in my duffel bag and hide the medicine bottle as I open it. *What the hell, I'm going to see what two of these do to me.*

I drop Finn off and head to my house, thankful that no one is home because I'm not feeling right as the Ritalin kicks in. I can feel my eyes ricocheting frantically around the garage as I pull in.

My Rottweiler, Bodhi, greets me at the door. Normally I'd roll around with him for a while, but I'm becoming panicked at some strange sensations and brush past him, just needing to get to bed. I chalk it up to the weight cut, but by the time I reach the third stair on my way up to my room, I realize that I can't feel my feet. I'm freaking out, place my hands on the carpet and continue on all fours. Once in my room, I pull off my shoes and see that my feet are purple. My heart is racing and begins pounding against my chest. I can hear it inside of my skull and out my ears. I lie down on my waterbed and bob up and down for a moment, wanting it all to stop. *Don't call mom . . . call mom . . . don't call mom.* I can't give myself up, can't tell anyone I've been taking the pills. I need to ride this out. I stare a hole in the ceiling. There's a shining pinpoint light and I'm convinced I'm seeing through time. I've opened a window in the continuum and am getting a small glimpse of something outside of us. It's fascinating. I love it. Myriad epiphanies stream through my consciousness. I push harder, trying to look, seeing something beyond here. I'm dying. I must be dying. A curiosity about that pinpoint window, that will never end, is hatched within me.

An hour later my brother screaming downstairs wakes me up. "Fuck you, I'm not going."

"You are too going!" My dad yells back.

My mouth is putrid and I'm so thirsty it hurts. Pins and needles crawl from head to toe and I feel as though I'm almost levitating. I take a scan, can feel my feet, and my heartbeat is normal - both improvements from an hour ago. Apart from the barren desert of my mouth, I feel surprisingly good and go to stretch. Everything in my arms and legs instantly cramps and I let out a little gasp, momentarily mummified. I relax, out of self-preservation, stopping it before it really knots up. Starting again I take it slowly, beginning with my fingers.

"What the hell is wrong with you?" I hear my dad yelling. Raleigh never came home last night and is . . . as unbelievable as it seems . . . on over a hundred hits of acid.

"There is nothing! NOTHING! Nothing wrong with me!" Raleigh shouts back. "Do you understand that? No. You don't! You will never understand it." Like I said, he's a beast and an intimidating physical figure. He has no qualms coming home and trying to start fistfights with my dad over the littlest issue. Things get out of hands sometimes - people can only take so much. My parents have been on the brink of sending him to military school for years, but just can't bring themselves to pull the trigger. I have no idea he's on drugs. I just think he's crazy. I'm a square compared to everyone else around this place, despite the levitating feeling of course. The whole town is on an endless trip; school days, mornings, weekends, it does not matter. They do not buy into a black and white world. There is a an alternate existence going on here like something out of Bradbury's Martian Chronicles. Like thermal imagery through a snake's eyes, the world really is what you see it to be and around here it's otherworldly, Technicolor and wide open. Parents who grew up with the "I Wanna Hold Your Hand" Beatles will never understand Sergeant Peppers. They will never understand the new world their children are creating in their minds. Right now I don't understand it either.

"Who's driving that car?" Knowing that he's in a losing battle, my dad now attempts to get practical and look out for his manic son's safety.

"Tom."

"Jesus. The Nelson Kid?" The resignation is heartbreaking. I can picture his exact facial expression as he throws his hands up above his shoulders and turns away from Raleigh, "Do what you want." The door closes a second later. Raleigh steals a couple of cans of beer our of the garage fridge before jumping back in Nelson's car, off to who knows where. I'm sure I'll see him later.

My dad watches through the front window as Raleigh tosses a beer can to his cohort. Even from a distance he can see Nelson is wild-eyed and in just as bad of shape, a crazed, freneticism emitting from the car like Hunter S. or Neal Cassidy. He watches as Nelson catches the beer with a twisted laugh, turns his head, throws the car in reverse and backing out of our long driveway too quickly, swerves all over ours and the neighbor's grass. It's broad daylight, kids are out circling the cul-de-sac on little bikes, and they'll be lucky not to kill someone as they careen out into the galaxy. My dad looks down at the phone in hand and starts to dial the police. 91 . . . and then he hangs up. He has no idea what is wrong with his son, but having spent sometime in a jail cell in his youth, he does not ever want to put his sons through that experience. Full of remorse, he puts the phone back down and starts up the stairs towards me.

I hear his footsteps creaking towards me. Without moving my body I turn to look, catching his eyes widen as they see me. I can't be a pretty site – all pasty skin and ribs.

"Are you OK?" He asks with genuine concern. I go to test my muscles again and have effectively eliminated the cramping. Slowly I rise.

"Cramps. I just need water."

He grabs my hand and helps me up, "Let's get over to the high school and get you on the scale."

Agent O'Riley throws a large 3-ring binder against a wall. It hits with a loud thud and slides down onto an impressive stack of file boxes; all marked "Harbor Files" in black Sharpie. The stack fills up one corner of the basement by where Agent Ramsey sits on a folding chair within arms reach of the papers. The plastic table in front of him is splayed with a dozen case files. Months of frustration are weighing down upon them. They've been going through case after case and taking notes for hours now. Time is running out and O'Riley paces relentlessly – pissed.

"I don't care what you have to do! I need to make an example of one of these little bastards." The implication is clear. Do what you have to do, whatever that entails. O'Riley's Judeo-Christian moralities begin to allow him to demonize these kids, his righteousness determining right and wrong to suits his needs. "We've got a month until graduation. If you can't get Waylon, I want to see you try and get as many 18 year olds as possible. I don't want the judges giving a bunch of bullshit juvie sentences and having the press make this whole thing look like we've been busting small time high school parties." He sits down across from Ramsey and rests his head on his hand, his index finger riding up above his temple and into his curly hair. He grabs a pen and quickly vibrates it back forth between his fingers to help his thinking. "Even if that's what the fuck we're doing."

"I think Nelson has a better chance at getting to Waylon at this point." Ramsey has had minimal success in the school and zero penetration into the major players. His haul has been small potatoes with a quarter of kind bud being the most anyone's been willing to sell him. Rumors of him being a narc have also been whispered about for a while now. This caused the Feds to toy with the idea, for about a month, of just pulling him completely. Ultimately they determined there was no danger and thought maybe his presence would be able to help deflect from Nelson in some way.

"I don't want to have to go through goddamn Chief Waters at all."

"There's no way around it Dan." Ramsey candidly gives him the truth. Nelson had actually brought them some real solid cases and although theoretically they should be pleased, any success came with numerous side effects, including worst of all, Chief Waters' gloating and continued involvement. They were simply tired of playing nice and pretending as though they were partners with him. He was the one who had brought them into this penny ante town and they were looking like fools for listening - unless something happened soon. "I think there could be some action tonight. We should push him." Ramsey says.

"Fine. Then push him. He's about to go off the fucking rails and then he won't be of any use to us anyways. We've got to wrap him up soon before he exposes us somehow. What's he say about Waylon?"

"He won't sell to him no matter what. Plays dumb, like he's got nothing to sell."

"Probably because he's so out of his mind. Waylon is smart to stay away from him."

"I know. I don't know what to do about it. He's deluded - convinced he's one of us. Thinks this is the beginning of his long career in the FBI."

"Even if we do get something out of him, we're going to have to send him somewhere to dry out in order to have him on the stand." O'Riley thinks out loud. "Goddamn Waters has given him a license to use every drug in the world and let him live out his little espionage fantasy."

"He's doing better than me." Ramsey shrugs his shoulders.

O'Riley lets his silence validate the truth of the statement, causing Ramsey to squirm in the awkward stillness. Continuing to read files, O'Riley methodically underlines and looks for connections, claws for a train of thought – some cohesion. He stops on a file and looks up at the ceiling, pondering. Through his brain run all sorts of barely legal, Patriot Act possible dynamics. Conversations gleaned from pay phones and back yard microphones. He chastises himself to think – to put it together. Something. This is how you made your career, what are you whining about? Think. Make this happen. Find the connection.

Ramsey gingerly flips through a file he has open before him and reluctantly begins to talk. "I've made a couple of buys from Sean Casper."

"Yeah. Small stuff though right?"

"Yeah. But he's been friends with Waylon since they played soccer together in the third grade."

"You think there's something there?"

"Could be." Ramsey says hesitantly. "I actually feel a little bad about the buys I made from him. I think he felt bad for everyone saying I was a narc and he just wanted to help me out."

"Why didn't you say something before?"

"He's a good kid." Shrugging his shoulders.

"There are no good kids in the drug game." O'Riley stares through him, telling him to get on with it.

Ramsey ignores the callousness of the statement. "Look at this." He's pointing out dates on Casper's file. "I've got 3 cases against Casper right? Each time I went to him," he pulls another file open with time stamped photos and Casper is seen in various poses, "we see Casper in Waylon's backyard. He definitely gets it from him. They go way back. Waylon trusts him." O'Riley's eyes widen. "And he turned 18 two weeks ago," he flips the file upside down to show him.

"So what? He's our possible way in how?"

"The real players, Waylon's tight clique, they're too smart and aware. There's a reason we don't have anything on them. We know they're moving large quantities, but we never see it. Don't know where it comes in, or where it goes. Casper on the other hand is a bit player. He's not really involved, but he is trusted by all of

56

them. He's a dreamer, always plotting get rich schemes. I think if we give him a plausible get rich quick story, put a giant billboard up with drum kits, surfboards, stereo systems and dollar signs . . . get him to go to Waylon. Who knows? Maybe he flips, or maybe we just get a big buy. I think he can get bulk if he really wants it and he might not be able to resist the thought of money."

"You've thought this through."

"Yes."

O'Riley nods as he analyzes the thoughts, momentarily sympathetic to the fact that Ramsey was protecting Casper. "O.K. Lets focus here and see how deep we can get this guy to go." Hopeful for the first time he can remember.

"Do you think we should tell Chief Waters anything?"

"No, let him go to the party tonight and start busting kids for dime bags. Idiot thinks he's Elliot Ness."

I've been in the bathroom for forty-five minutes, sitting on the toilet and drinking a six-pack of lukewarm Busch. A towel is wrapped around my waist and I am still a bit wet from the long shower I had taken. Droplets of water occasionally run down my sides and over my stomach, which is extended and plush with too much food and liquid. Ten minutes ago, my mother checked on me but I played it off like I was upset and needed to be alone. I stare out into the gray sky through an open window, my third beer sliding down my throat and a cool breeze touching my face, making the world feel real. Some random birds chatter and I find myself hopeful they've come north, bringing with them some signal of spring. A second later I'm wondering whether they've braved it out through the winter, but realize quickly the only thing I'm really concerned with is getting a good buzz going. My watch tells me Finn should be walking over here in about 20 minutes. I'll drink one more in my solitude and sneak the final two out of the house in my waistband.

I lost my match earlier today to some kid I'd beaten easily 3 times before. Sure I had put on 22 lbs. before I stepped onto the mat, but I had nothing in the gas tank, an insurmountable weakness in my arms and legs. To top that off, I made it to the gym and realized I had left the Ritalin in my room and could not think of a good enough excuse to tell my dad why I had to run back home. I don't know if it would've helped anyways, I was so drained. I sulked my way off the mat, acting, more than being, genuinely disappointed, playing my role in the theater of the inconsequential. Half a crowded gym was in silent shock at my loss and the other half was busy losing their minds over a victory they never imagined. I was just so bored with it all. The inhumane amount of pressure to perform I've been under for the last 10 years is coming to an end. I hide the happiness of being one week closer to high school sports being done forever. My parents and coaches think I'll be wrestling in college, but I know better. I know that as soon as I'm out of their view . . . I'll be gone.

Looking past the hundreds of disappointed stares from my side of the gym, I scanned the crowd for Poppy's dark eyes, registering the shell-shocked look of my father and younger brother in the middle of the stands, their proud moment morphing into shame. I turn away from them and find Poppy's crazy hair and wild clothes tucked away up in the corner, popping out vividly from the masses. She is the opposite everything happening in this gym, a vortex of dark calm and rationality. Her husky-white eyes pierce mine and I know she knows what I'm thinking. *Who cares, it's all a charade.* It helps as I collapse onto the folded chair and watch Finn destroy his opponent. I'm happy to cheer him on, but after that, I'm just going through the motions.

NOW - the droplets on my skin mix with the cool air, feeling like rebirth. I'm coming out of a weeklong fast and catching a buzz quickly. The tingling is everywhere; my lips curl up at the corners. I'm relieved to be done with it all for a couple of days and feel good - right now. I'm becoming aware that I love nothing more than intoxication; it is an adventure into the unknown, riding the pure thought of infinity out to the edge of space to look over the edge. A long line of drinkers, mostly Irish with a little bit of Cherokee, have bred to create me. *Irish and Native American- yes I was born to drink,* I think to myself. I drink not because it's in my blood. I drink for the love it. Because it opens portals and shows me world I never would see otherwise. It allows my ego to wander, to visualize, to dream and swim in a world we've only read about in books. I drink because it makes me want to tell stories that make everything better. I drink because I feel as though I can be anything my mind imagines. I am not here right now. I am somewhere that does not actually exist.

KNOCK! KNOCK! KNOCK!

"Crazy boy Finn is here." My mother says jokingly. She loves the kid too.

"All right, tell him I'll be down in two."

Finn and Annie, Poppy and I bounce along in my car, the four of us circling The Center hunting for someone to get us beer, my patience lowering with each empty can. "Fuck it, let's go downtown." I say spinning the wheel and heading towards the highway. It's a twenty-minute drive and we have two semi-reliable places that allow us to use our ridiculous fake ID's. We tell no one of these spots. That mistake was made once, resulting in us blowing up our own spot when a bunch of brainless, white-ass shitballs started acting like they knew something. Last thing any shop owner wants is you telling a bunch of idiots that you'll sell beer to minors. Tonight, I'm going to drive a little further to my second option because the last time I went to the one over on 44th there was an armed robbery on the joint when I was leaving. I saw it start to happen in the circular, reflective mirror. A convexed, young kid in a gray hoodie pulled a gun at the counter. I took off to a pay phone down the street to call 911. I like the Pakistani guy who owns the place, even though I don't really know what he's saying - ever. He has a good natured laugh and I've discerned he thinks it's hilarious we drink Mad Dog 20 / 20 and Night Train - Boones Farm for the girls - the same cheap wines the hobos drink. I drove by later and saw him in there so I know he wasn't hurt, but I haven't been back inside to buy beer from him yet. I'm hoping I don't have to go back there and just pray that it's a clerk I know at the second spot, which we normally reserve as a backup.

I get off the highway an exit later and we take a right onto West 25th heading into a decrepit neighborhood of battered chain link fences, boarded up windows and rotting frames. The store is a dark little hole in the wall in a barren wasteland of cracked asphalt. I don't remember how we found this place, except that it had to do with one of my favorite skateboard shops being fairly close by. I assume we were just driving around trying various bodegas until we got lucky.

Old wind chimes, tied to a string, mark my entrance into the shop. The owner is a bit more shady and suspicious, but tonight it's his son on duty and I've never had a problem with him. He's watching some Korean TV show that's static half the time.

Somehow, he's pulling it in over the rabbit ears. As I stroll through the aisles, avoiding eye contact and keeping myself out of sight until it's necessary, he's laughing at some prank show. They have some wine coolers in stock tonight, so I grab some for the girls as a special little treat they'll be happy about. I grab Finn and I four bottles of MD 20/20 and a two-liter cooler for myself just to have something sweet and easy to drink later in the night. The son watches me approach the counter, knowing he has the power to ruin my night.

"How are you?" I say nonchalant. He squints a bit, nods and does not even ask for my ID. He's good that way. I don't actually know why any of these clerks have us go through the charade of showing these 4-dollar state ID's we got in some trinket shop in the mall. I may be 17, but look 15 and no matter how much I puff up my muscles, no one is mistaking me for a grown man - although I secretly hope they are. The cash register rings out and I get a rush from the transaction.

We're in business and in a hurry to get back to familiar grounds with our loot when I cut off a car a little too close and accidentally piss off some hoods in a suped-up Nova next to us. I can see their faces turn in the rearview mirror as they realize it's a couple of white kids, with their little girlfriends, seemingly lost in the wrong neighborhood. They start pushing on their gas and trying to come up alongside of us as I block their way. This goes on for a minute or so before Finn is the first to realize I'm playing a cat and mouse game. He looks in the side mirror and sees them yelling through their windshield.

"Oh shit, they look pissed." He says turning around fully.

"Yeah," I respond, mad that he called it out. I'd been trying to play it cool in order to keep the girls from noticing, but now they're all looking out the back window as though mass murderers are chasing us. Their faces of fear feed the fire of our pursuers who now fully realize what they have in front of them, giving them more reason to continue the pursuit. Evil intentions or not, it'll just be fun for them to terrorize us.

Tires screeeeeching, they weave back and forth recklessly behind us, attempting to come alongside as the girls scream. I'm watching my mirrors and adrenaline is coursing through me. I smile inside, enjoying this, confident of my driving skills. Only slight a fear crystalizes my mind. At the last second, I spin around a corner and it takes them a moment to recover while I fly down a side street and rip a left onto 44th, a main street, and head towards the biggest intersection I know in the area. I have a 10-house lead on them, but it's not good enough to lose them. The light ahead of us is green and I let off the gas trying to time the yellow light. Finn and the girls feel our momentum stop and scream, "What are you doing? Go! Go!" The car gets closer as I watch the light. *Still green, come on.* I come to a stop just as the light turns yellow. The hoods slam on their breaks behind us as the chorus of screams reaches full panic. I watch the light turn red and wait . . . one more second . . . and then at the last moment, just as the cross traffic starts, I peel out across the intersection, trapping our pursuers behind the flow.

"Jesus Christ!" Finn yells.

I'm laughing hysterically and can't believe it worked. "I saw that move in a Eddie Murphy movie," I yell immensely pleased with myself. The adrenaline dump sends a warm, nirvanic calm over my body. I feel awake and alive staring at the blank page of the night before us. We turn onto the highway and head back towards the burbs.

"I can't do it anymore man. I'm gonna go up to 152." It's the weight class above Finn and it makes sense since I don't want to wrestle him off and he's guaranteed to win states where he is. So I'll go the weight class above him and try to get my strength back.

"Yeah man, you've always been stronger than everyone, you might as well use it."

"Plus I can drink more." Only half joking as my face grimaces from the swig of grape liquor. I get past it's nastiness quick.

I park a street a little ways over from the party, just in case we need to make a stealth exit later, and we walk the extra couple of blocks to Waylon's house. There are cars up and down the street, smartly separated as to not give away whose house everyone is visiting. I see my brother, Raleigh, carrying a 12-pack walk into the house with Nelson and hope he's in a better mood. After their little brush with street life the girls chugged through a couple of wine coolers on the ride and are feeling giddy about being back in their safe haven. Grabbing Poppy by the hand, the thought of sneaking her up into one of the bedrooms later for some alone time takes root. She squeezes mine back and with a look lets me know she's reading my mind.

The music is pounding through the house and it's hard to make our way through the crowd. Nelson is barreling his way around the room, spilling beer out of a clear Solo cup onto people milling about. He's out of his mind, desperately trying to hold onto the earth and ricocheting aimlessly. He stumbles a bit and tries to clasp onto some freshman girls. No one here would realize the weight of the world bearing down on his twisted head. It drives him further into his intoxication. *There's no way those fucking Feds could go back on their deal. Right? Shit. I can get Casper. If I can't get Waylon, I can get Casper.* His attempt to rationalize setting up his childhood friends only confuses him more. Dark thoughts spin towards the back of his brain until they dissolve into a compartment of self-loathing. He is a broken human, a psyche torn in two, working up the strength, or whatever it is that makes a snitch a snitch.

Until this afternoon he'd been into the intrigue of it all, trying to embrace his role with the police, a kernel of his brain enjoying himself as an undercover agent. No one was gonna get hurt. It had all been pretend, a TV version of his life clouded inside a concoction of booze and pills. He inhaled any drug which came his way and chalked it up to being part of the job, part of the role he's playing. It helped his performance. He gulps down giant swigs of beer and throws his hands through his sweaty hair, looking around for someone, anyone. He sees Agent Ramsey awkwardly drinking from a plastic cup in the corner of the room and they lock eyes. Ramsey's presence infuriates him and sends him bouncing back off through the crowd. It's him or someone else. Gotta make the case. *I'm a fucking rat. I will be a rat for life.*

People are making out in nooks and crannies. In the kitchen kids holding balloons are laughing hysterically around a nitrous tank while some sophomore football player, I sort of know, frantically rifles through the cupboards looking for munchies. Off in a little side room some stoners are giggling hysterically at themselves while blowing smoke in Waylon's dog's ear. "Fucking cut it out." I yell at them. They look up surprised and apologize as Spencer sees me and trots over. I rub his head and snap my fingers for him to follow me. We make it to the back stairs and start down to the crawlspace.

A couple of college kids are making their way back up the stairs and out towards the night. With glazed eyes, they look at me in disbelief - everything is an illusion. Apparently unaccustomed to the strength of the product, they hold onto the walls and suppress bursts of laughter, at war with themselves about whether things can really be as absurd as they seem. I walk past a few girls in the corner of the basement scheming about who they're going to hook up with. Inside the crawlspace Waylon is holding marijuana court, perfectly stoned and judiciously passing the bong. It's been a long day and a winding journey to reach the sanctuary. The soft squeeze of the bass from the music upstairs is muffled through the cement walls and tapestries and feels like bumps of serene silence. Strings of light shine softly and snake along the walls while the outside world disappears.

"Tough one today." Waylon says, his head leaning back against the wall.

"Fuck it. I just want it all to be over."

"I think tonight's the night." Finn chimes in laughing. He puts a joint in front of my face. Poppy looks on, half urging me, half waiting her turn. I look at it and decide to take it. It's a visceral feel of paper and flame and small leaves in my mouth. I hold it in for too long and let out a huge cough. Everyone laughs and I smile too. I take another drag and hand it over to Poppy who is looking at me knowingly. It's hydroponic, perfected by a million connoisseurs, and does not take long to ride through me. A moment of turbulence followed by joy. I get a wave of déjà vu that sticks extraordinarily long. The world seems to stop around me and I put my hands out to steady myself. I exhale slowly to calm down, know I've been here before and KNOW there's no such thing as time. I'm amazed by the epiphany and scan the eyes of everyone around me to determine if anyone else knows this. It's momentous. Should I keep it a secret? They all stare at me and I stare back and them, eyes bugging out of my head. Simultaneously everyone busts out laughing at me. I'm in shock, unsure these monkeys are real and then I just start laughing hysterically with them. All walls and constraints are shattered. I will never believe the news or authorities again, the ones who told me this is bad for me. It's all a lie. I am overwhelmed by the newness of my life, by the beauty of each second. I am amazed to be here on this planet, a tiny speck in a small basement in the corner of the universe. I'm watching the movie of my life happen before me. I laugh and smoke for hours as people climb in an out of the crawl space. I am in the know, part of the collective unconsciousness.

At some point, Raleigh crawls in, smiles at me and nods as though I've joined his celestial mystery. "Hello big brother." He says in a knowing tone. I freak out for a second at the thought that there's been an entire world existing along side of me for my entire life. I get the overwhelming feeling of a million realities happening simultaneously. I think of aliens watching us, I think that there must be people from the future who have figured out time travel and they must be the aliens and then I'm scrambling out of the crawlspace and up the stairs, through the doors and outside into the starry night. The Milky Way stretches in a white line over the treetops. I'm following it to its end when I feel Poppy take my hand. I turn to her and she is beautiful, separated from the air by a subtle tiny aura I've never seen before. She appears to be cut out of the night and floating before me. I will never forget this sight. We are two time travelers soaring through the universe on this journey together. I watch the trees breathe the night in deeply and join them.

Down in the basement, Nelson is resting his hand on the doorframe leading to the stairwell, barely able to support himself, slurring badly and has momentarily trapped Waylon from going upstairs. Swaying back and forth he says, "Listen, we've got to talk."

"Get the fuck out of here, you're spitting all over the place. Go the fuck home man." Waylon goes to move past him and Nelson stops him by putting his hand on his chest. This is not a smart move as Waylon already has the instincts of a Godfather. He backs up and glares as his face burns red. Casper comes up and steps between.

"Come on man, come with me for a minute." He ushers his friend up the stairs. A couple of girls coo over Waylon at the bottom of the stairs, petting his puffed chest and telling him it's all right.

"That prick . .. that prick . . . he's got some shit coming to him." Nelson is slurring as Casper pushes him up towards the music. He leads Nelson all the way outside and I see him steer him over to the side of the garage with some gentle nudges. I follow their saga until they disappear.

Casper pushes Nelson up against the siding between two little Juniper trees. "What the fuck is wrong with you? Come on man, you got to get it together."

"I'm sorry man, I'm sorry. I was just trying . . . it's just that . . . I . . ."

"You what? Jesus talk dude."

Conflicted, Nelson looks at Casper with blurry, diluted eyes. Somewhere in the back of his brain neurons fire, triggering memories of childhood sleepovers. He knows he can make this happen. Knows all he has to do is ask. Pangs of deep pity and remorse churn his insides. If it were Waylon he wouldn't care, Waylon has it coming to him eventually. But Casper is just an innocent. He's tried to avoid implicating anyone he was remotely friendly with, but Agent Ramsey made it clear what he had to do.

"It's just that . . . I just want to talk to Waylon . . . I got this deal."

"What deal?" "It'd be better if you just get Waylon to talk to me, man." It's a last ditch effort to save Casper.

"He doesn't want to talk to you. And now," He looks back towards the house, "he really doesn't want to talk to you."

Nelson drops his head and leans back against the garage, defeated.

"Just tell me what it is. Maybe I can tell him." Casper offers.

"My dad cut me off." His drunken brain trying to keep straight the story he made up this afternoon with Ramsey, "He's not gonna pay for me to go to this training camp in Vegas I was supposed to go to. I got a chance to get away, maybe go pro, but he won't help me out anymore." He reaches the limit of his acting ability and drops some truth into the scene, "I need to get out of this town man. I can't go work for him, or be one of these flunkies hanging around the Center."

"So what you think? Waylon's gonna give you money?" Casper is unable to conceive that he would even think that an option.

"No man." Shaking his head. "There's these guys down at the gym and they got some connections, you know. I got a way for me to make some real money. If I could just get my hands on some quantity, I could get rid of it real fast." He hesitates and lays it on.

71

"We could make some REAL money man." He stares into Casper's eyes, not knowing what to feel. He's happy with his performance while simultaneously hoping it does not work.

Casper's brain rapid fires a hundred tangential thoughts, flashes of his obsessions and tagged pages in magazines, desired wants – destinations and things, things, things. Visions of new turntables, a surfboard and a remote control airplane swim around the back of his eyeballs. All the knockoffs his parents bought him, not realizing they were mere facsimiles of the real thing, everything he can't afford. Teenage fantasies. "What kind of money?"

I'm standing in the yard feeling my feet take root once again. My skull is pulling it's self back together and a mindful understanding and appreciation takes over my present. In a flash of synchronicity, or cosmic awareness, I look between the trees lining the wooden framed houses at the end of the street and happen to see a couple of squad cars creeping slowly around the block.

"Let's go." I grab Poppy and run over to the small basement window and push it open. "The cops are here!"

In an instant, Waylon is expertly sweeping up all paraphernalia, places it into a hidden hole in the wall and flicks a switch, setting off a fan that blows the air out of the windows. Hanging up the painting that covers the crawlspace entrance, he barks orders to hide the nitrous tank and then marches up the stairs to deal with the police.

"COPS!!!!" I yell into the night. The word ping pongs through the party as Poppy and I take off across the street and through the backyards in the opposite direction the police will expect anyone to run. Finn magically appears next to us with Annie in tow. He and I are connected at the brain, years of eluding these situations providing us with the instinctual escape route. We duck behind a house and watch just as the cruisers pull up out front and turn their lights on. It's like watching lions catch zebra calves on the Discovery channel as all the weak ones, frozen by flashlight beams, stop dead in their tracks. We see Casper breaking through the backyard and make it to a tree line by the creak and know he's in the clear.

A bunch of cops are spread out across the yards, one of them, a little older stands out from the rest. He barks out quick directions as the three others round up stragglers and section off groups of teenagers. Little yellow notepads are pulled out and one by one they flip the pages, taking down names and phone numbers - far too eager to start calling parents and have these criminals picked up to get their just dessert. Waylon has appeared in the doorway and the officer in charge approaches him. His presence does nothing to stop the officer from entering as he brushes past Waylon with disdain. Once inside, the first thing the cop sees is Nelson passed out on a couch. The officer knows all about him and gives a disgusted grunt before tapping him on the forehead with a flashlight. It does not faze him so he brings the light down harder a second time. "Get out of here." The officer says with an authoritative growl. Nelson breaks from the blackness of his sleep, flailing at his unseen attacker. With a pain in his forehead, he tries to squint up at him at the cloudy image but the room is immediately in full spin and any more movement feels as though it will surely result in his death. The officer recognizes the possibility of vomit ending up all over him and simply moves on towards the kitchen. "Anyone else in here?" He says to Waylon.

"No, he's it." Waylon is watching him and relieved when he does not open the corner pantry and discover the 4-foot high nitrous tank.

"I'm sure if I start taking things apart in here, I'm gonna find some stuff to so you might as well tell me where your stash is." He's flicking on lights in the bedrooms.

"Everyone brought their own beer."

The officer knows Waylon is being a smart ass, but unless he feels like searching this entire place at midnight on Friday without sufficient probable cause, he's not going to be able to make him pay for it. "Where's your dad at?"

"Out for the night."

"He know you're having this little shindig?"

"No." It's a lie.

"Heh," he grunts. "Well, I'm sure he'll be really happy when he's in court for this." The officer walks back past Waylon and out the front door, throwing a subtle shoulder at him in the process. He'll let the patrolman handle the situation from here and maybe make it home in time for his own little nightcap.

I see him exit from across the street and a moment later Waylon's silhouette appears back in the doorway. *Not being led out in handcuffs is always a good thing.* The crisp sound of beer can cracking open grabs my ear. I turn to see a big smile break across Finn's face and reach my hand out. He grabs another beer from the remainder of 12-pack he brought with him and hands it over. "Last One." He says with the shared implication that something must be done about that.

It's a perfect fall night and we make a calm exit through the backyard to the next street where our car is parked. Behind us angry parents begin arriving beneath the streetlights, all hot and bothered with the indignity of impending gossip to come. My pot high is giving way to the old familiar alcohol buzz and I feel as though I'm reaching the end of an excursion and stepping back through a rip in the cosmos I never knew was there. I've made an evolutionary stride, a realization from which I'll never be the same, but I need time to process and now just want the cold comfort of some beer and leave the Stargate of the new world hovering in the blue night behind me.

We reach the car having already run through the possibility of sneaking into our respective houses and swiping some booze from our parents. Ultimately deciding that running the inherent risk of a shortened night - by being caught - is not worth it. We scrounge for some money, but it won't be enough to get us what we need, so yahooing it is. There's a Dairy Mart I know of out by the airport and although its in a pretty sketchy area next to the projects - for some reason it appeals to me - a foreign land with the least chance of happening to run into someone who will recognize me. Annie is already late, so we need to drop her off, but Poppy says she can come, which is crucial, because at this point Finn is too fucked up to either drive or run, so I'll need her for my getaway driver.

It's an uneventful fifteen-minute drive back down the highway. A little fog forms in the air and I can see particles floating like atoms. They fly past me as I race down the highway watching the painted lines and funneling through them like some space racing video game, the opening text of Star Wars. Only when I get off the exit do I notice a cruiser behind me. I'm about 12 beers and some Mad Dog into the night, but the danger hones my senses further and I flick on the right blinker, slow to a perfectly executed stop, wait the allotted three seconds and proceed south towards the airport. *All normal here officer.* He continues in the opposite direction and I smile my invincible smile.

The Dairy Mart sits on a corner with it's big, blue and white sign shining into the night and flooding the dilapidated parking lot with light. It's an oasis in the darkness. A little side street runs along its North side and a single street light flickers on the corner, fading out quickly down the block. The darkness will provide further cover. I turn down there and park the car about 10 houses down, enough to use my speed to keep the clerk from seeing my car clearly and providing a description. We stop and play a little musical chairs with Poppy jumping into the driver seat and Finn taking over the passenger seat. This will enable me to dive headlong into the back seat on my escape.

I've only done this once before and it was a frightening experience when sober, but I'm clouded at this point, half of me knowing I could pass out now if I tried - and half of me, as always, just wanting the night to never end. So with the thought of seeing the sunrise pinpointing in my head, I walk towards the store - stomach turning. It's a badly lit b-movie upon entering, fluorescent lights shining off the waxed linoleum floor. The perfectly stocked shelves seem unreal as I look up at the Middle Eastern owner behind the counter and quickly look away. He doesn't like the sight of me in this part of town, at this time of night. He doesn't like the way my eyes looked away. There's a sway to my walk and he's on alert as I approach the beer cooler. Having made up my mind to carry through the plan I don't notice any of this. I'm on a kamikaze mission, mind controlled by the tunneled vision voice of alcohol – the Demon as my dad likes to call it.

I grab a couple of 12 packs of Old Milwaukee and walk back towards the counter one aisle closer to the door than any normal patron would. I realize this and pretend I'm looking for something amongst the random selection area of the aisle; gloves, WD-40, tampons, saltines, tweezers. My eyes cloud and I lose my sense of equilibrium for a moment. Steadying myself, I act as though I don't see what I'm looking for and make my way towards the clerk. This action calms him for he thinks he is just left with a choice of selling to an obviously underage kid or not. It's a tough call this time of night – I'm obviously drunk, probably not sent by the police and it could be a little more money in the register. I can see his internal dialogue playing out on his brow. If I had any money on me right now, I'd just try to buy these. But I don't. The cardboard handles feel tactile on my fingers as I grip them. I get a vague sensation of adrenaline seeping out through the numbness in my limbs. Pull focus from the blur. Try to hone my senses again, Take a strong step towards him. Look him in the eye.

"Yahoooooo!!!!" - I yell drunkenly as I break towards the door.

I'm through smooth, fast as fuck considering my impairment. I see the brake lights come on as I sprint towards my car. The reverse lights shine white momentarily and I know Poppy is ready to pull out.

"STOP! STOP! I SHOOT!" I turn to see the clerk yelling at me in a thick Middle Eastern accent. Beneath the store sign in the parking lot behind me he's showered in a seemingly glittery volume of light, particles of dust sand dirt float around him. I see his eye tracking me over the rifle he's aiming at me. THE WORLD IS CLEAR. I turn back towards my car instantaneously thinking he can't shoot me. I'm about to cut across the tree lawn to dive into the backseat when CRACK. The rifle rings out in the night. At the same time, I assume someone has bashed me across the back of the head with a baseball bat. Whiplashed, my head flies forward and I'm sent sailing through the air. Beer cans go flying in front of me, bouncing off the sidewalk, shrapnel spraying into the ghetto. The second twelve pack lands right in front of my face - intact. I look to my left, my car 4 feet from me. Finn's face is pressed flat against the passenger side window. His eyes bulge, his mouth is agape. I can feel the texture of the cement grating against my chest. There is a quiet stillness in the air. With disbelief, I press my hands on the ground, get to my knees, grab the twelve pack and jump into the back seat as Poppy peels away.

"FUCK, FUCK, FUCK." I'm screaming and grabbing the back of my head. Poppy spins a left and gets us out of harms way. "Turn on the light." I yell to Finn. He does so as I rip off my brown, leather jacket. I instantly see what appears to be water stains darkening the leather. It takes a second to register that it's blood. The back seat too is stained and I stop rubbing my head and just press against it. I'm alive, but I don't know why. Having grown up next to the train tracks, my only experience with guns were the salt guns the railroad men would shoot from the cabooses to keep us from climbing aboard the trains. So I'm thinking salt gun. That's what must have happened. It's helping the panic. Poppy is already back on the highway and we're 10 minutes from her house. None of us know what to say. I'm trying to stop the bleeding with my hands and can feel my hair soaking up and beginning to mat. I can't go to the hospital and tell them I was robbing a store. I can't go home and be by myself. We decide that I'll go to Finn's house. He has his own little section of the place on the first floor. Once he makes sure his parents are asleep, he'll sneak me in the backdoor. Poppy parks my car a around the bend from the house and says she can walk from there. I have no time for chivalry.

She's in a state of shock, "Call me tonight. You promise."

"Promise. I'll be fine." And reach my lips out for a kiss, careful to keep blood off of her. She heads off and I give a reassuring wave. My brain is overloaded, chemicals flying to the end of my neurons and sizzling, the entire situation dreamlike and overwhelming. It's causes my inebriation to spin outside of my head. I have the sensation of floating off into the ether and feel a little ill. Finn leads me towards his place, the night air helping me slightly. He enters through a backdoor and I lean against his house, staring out into the green black darkness of the meticulously landscaped yard. Chemical rushes are sweeping over my head and I'm battling bursts of fear. I've been shot. I could be dying. I need reassurance from somewhere but know it will not come. Instead, impending doom blankets me and I just want to get into a hot shower for some comfort, get this blood off of me and fall asleep.

The door opens a minute later and Finn leads me in to the dark house. I've been here a million times and have no problem finding my way through the mudroom. Stripping down to my underwear, I carry my clothes into the bathroom and lay them on the tile floor where I'll be able to clean up any mess. Finn follows me in. His eyes pop open with shock at the sight of me. "Jesus. You need anything?"

My reflection catches me in the mirror and I see dried blood all over my ears and cheeks, it drips down my neck and chest. "Not right now."

"You think we should go to the hospital?"

"I don't think so."

"All right," he's at a loss, "I'll be in my room." The door closes and he quickly heads off. I can hear the TV flick on as I turn on the hot water and step in. Steam fills the room. I plunge my face upwards into the stream and run my hands gingerly through my hair, getting it clean before I dare to probe the hole in my head. *What is this?* Just above where my skull stops and connects with my spine there are two holes in the back of my head, one on each side. *Two holes?* I can stick my index finger in them fairly deep. It frightens and baffles me. I agree with my earlier diagnosis of salt gun, otherwise I'd be dead right? With this thought, and all of the blood off of me, I feel better. Stepping out of the shower to dry myself off, the blood starts to flow again. I find a large washcloth and tie it around my head bandana style. Finn stares at me as I walk into his room like this.

"Well?"

"I'm just going to go to sleep."

"You don't want to go home?" I can see he's afraid that I will die in his house. What would he do if he woke up next to his best friend, dead? Understandable.

"I'll be fine." I lay down with my head on the bottom end of his bed and instantly pass out into blackness.

The pounding in my head is intense. A hangover like I've never had before. Pushing myself up, I realize I cannot turn my head. Gingerly touching the bullet holes, there's a swelling that was not there the night before. It's as though a tunnel as developed between the two holes, it's tender to the touch and the pain worries me. The clock says 10:41 and in a panic I remember my little brother is wrestling downtown in an hour. He's trying to become a 4-time city champ. It's a big deal, and has only happened once before, years ago. I can feel my parent's wondering where the hell I am, their anger growing. The pressure clamps down on me as I pull myself from bed, gravity multiplied a thousand times.

"Hey." I shake Finn. "'We've got to go to cities man. I need some clothes." With his eyes closed he points at his dresser. "Get up." I say. "Let's go."

"How are you?" He grumbles.

"Something's not right with my head. I think it's infected. I'll figure it out later." I say digging through his drawers. "Coach is going to be looking for us and my parents are gonna be pissed. I never called them last night." I put some socks on as he shuffles towards the bathroom, rubbing his eyes.

The backseat of my car is stained with blood and I throw the clothes I've wrapped in a plastic bag on top of it, still unable to comprehend the situation. Finn has looked at my head and confirmed it's swelling pretty badly. "I think the bullet must have gone in one side and come out the other." He tells me. The doctor will later confirm via x-ray that I had turned my head just enough for the bullet to skim my skull, ricochet at a slight direction and go out the other side. "2 Inches lower and it would have gone through your spine, 4 degrees less of a turn and it would have gone into your skull." He looks at me in disbelief. "You're extremely lucky." I'm glad I made that turn towards my car when I did, but all I know right now is that I need to go to a doctor and come up with a story for my parents that does not involving me stealing anything.

The gym is a hive of pep talks and stress, filled with thousands of people in the crevices of old wooden auditorium stands. Children bounce in warm up suits with headphones on, slapping their own faces, psyching themselves up. Grunting loudly, yelling. Fathers pace anxiously, envisioning this to be the entirety of their children's future. High school coaches are here watching. There are pathways to college scholarships here RIGHT NOW if you can only find them, if your kid can only perform.

I have Finn walk ahead of me to deflect any overeager parents wondering about whether I'm going to be able to make my weight loss work. "Rough match last time. Looked tired. You think you'll be able to keep your strength at 135?" All very important, fate of the world stuff. We spot my parents and begin stepping up the wooden planks, zigzagging between families. We know most everyone and they all know us. The same statewide wrestling circles, for over ten years now, breeds familiarity. We skip with pity past the families with hopeless children, the type you wish to be matched against for an easy route to the finals of any tournament. We feel the ire of parents whose kids are close, but not quite close enough to beating us. We step past the mothers and fathers of our rivals and take the daggers of their barely hidden, death stares of disdain. Grown men despise us. Fucking losers. I am thankful for all the things I am not and all the things I will never be. They hope I won't be able to keep up the weight loss. They love the fact that I lost an easy match and whisper amongst themselves that I'm done - vulnerable. Welcome to high school.

Speaking of death stares . . . my mother has spotted us. She can see that something is wrong with me, but my health is not currently her concern. She's irate. A couple of weeks ago she had come bursting into a gym where I was wrestling after receiving a call from some parents claiming I had shaved their fur coats during a party, drained their above ground swimming pool, after throwing the lawnmower in and turned their car sideways in the driveway to trap it between two houses. I only done one of those things - but she came in like a bat out of hell, found Finn and I in a nanosecond and violently pointing to us into the stands, ordered us telepathically to follow her out of the building. We did not give up the real culprits, but she did go through my car looking for some items the mother claimed I had and in turn found a few dozen empty Old Milwaukee cans in my hatchback. Moral of the story being, she is in no mood for another scene in the stands - amongst these people.

"Where the hell were you?" She growls in a deep-throated low voice.

Sitting one rung below her, and turned awkwardly towards her, I stammer, still trying to think of what I'm going to tell her. "I fell asleep and forgot to call."

She's staring at me now. "What is wrong with you?"

On the spot, I decide to go with shock to twist her anger into concern. "I was shot last night."

"What?" She shakes her head. It does not register, her eyes narrow. "What are you talking about?" She does not accept the reality shift.

"In the back of the head. I was at a party and some girl's brother came home and he started chasing everybody out of the house with a gun." I wasn't lying yet; this did happen a couple of months ago.

Finn is nodding along. That did happen, he's impressed. The fact that we have not yet lied helps the sincerity on our faces and the cracks in the story my mother would normally spot are not there. "So this kid shot you? And we didn't hear from the police?" Her anger is properly diverted as my father is doing his own zigzag to reach us. He's more annoyed with me upsetting my mother than he is about not calling, but when he realizes my high school wrestling career is over his world will fall apart. My mother whispers the story into his year. He's scanning me over as she talks and assessing my mobility – processing - hoping I'm not hurt bad – for a number of reasons. Processing. There's no time for this now as my brother is on deck. He gives one last look at me, his pupils ripping through me. The real story will come to light soon enough, but for now we turn towards the mat and watch my little brother make some local history.

Gliding past barren office complexes, with oversized "For Lease" signs, agents O'Riley and Ramsey drive their government issued, dark black Chevy Caprice down Frontage Road. They turn into a drive and up to an entrance of a single story, sprawling, brown brick building. The extra large font declares the address on the top of the building '22905'. It's circular entrance and thin windows hint at faux 70's architecture. Pulling around back they park next to Bob Nelson's very sweater around the neck, convertible Mercedes.

"Jesus Christ, look at the snot coming out of your nose. You're a mess." Disgusted, Bob Nelson chastises his son. Tom rubs his nose, looks down and his hand and is just relieved it's not blood. Behind his head streaming lines of cars paint the spaces between a thin smattering of trees and a grassy hill separating the complex from the highway that runs along the entire corridor. The Nelson's lock eyes with the agents as they pull in.

They all exit their cars simultaneously. It's a sloppy way to meet in the middle of the day, but they'll see anyone before being seen. O'Riley uses a key to enter the building and they all walk through it's bluish white halls. Speckled grey-blue carpet connects to the walls by blue plastic baseboards. The building's past hints of doubling for doctor's offices and wanna-be accounting services, among other numerous short-lived ventures. A couple of fluorescent lights flicker and lead them towards an old wooden door with Gold plated lettering 'Brookes Financial'.

Inside the office is a table with some folding chairs, a few computers, a small fridge, a coffee machine and some old beige aluminum cabinet files, their dents spraying the bad lighting in all directions. This is their staging area away from Chief Waters' prying eyes. They all sit down with a familiarity from having met here a half a dozen times before. O'Riley is pissed and does not wait to dive in. "How was the party last night Tom?" Tom's bloodshot eyes are floating in dark circles and his head is pounding. "Chief Waters tells me you were passed out and the officers couldn't wake you?" Bob Nelson lowers his head, disgusted with his son. *Will this ever end?*

"I was sleeping." Their looks tell him that they're not buying it and he needs to divert them with some good news quickly before this goes south on him. "Whatever. I set up a big buy for this week." He embellishes the situation a bit and leans back in his chair as though he doesn't give a shit - and at this point he really doesn't.

"Casper?"

Tom just nods and sinks deeper into his chair. Setting up an innocent to save his own hide is stoking his apathy. He needs to detach from it all in order to carry this whole thing through. They've made him believe he's failed and the only way out is to take this path. Every time he feels like he can't get any lower, he's surprised to find a new bottom again.

"Of what?"

"I'll figure that out with him today. I told him we'd talk about how we can each make the most money. But he'll do it. He'll make it happen"

"I want to see if he can get heroin." O'Riley says bluntly in a way that makes Bob Nelson's head pop up and Tom slide up a bit in his chair. He looks to his dad for some backing. *Come on this is too much.*

"Heroin? Is there a heroin problem in this town?" Bob Nelson is aghast.

"No, not right now, but we need to know if there's access, because if there is . . . eventually there will be a problem." Technically, it's a true statement, but it's not the reason he wants a heroin buy to be made. Heroin will make the headlines. Heroin will get him funding. SUBURBAN KIDS SHOOTING UP is one of the last images anyone wants in their brains. Part of his request however is pure curiosity. They've essentially been unable to penetrate Waylon's veil at all and tracing heroin's trail could help tell him more about the supply chain. It's the legitimate thoughts that make him feel better about himself. "At least ask. See what he thinks about it. Tell him there's more money in that and cocaine, psychedelics next, but no marijuana." Bob Nelson watches his sons face for signs of reality. What is possible? What is his son into? His nose still running, Tom knows that there's everything imaginable in this town, but until this point he had avoided trying for anything more than weed. He figured no one was going to get into that much trouble for weed. The blackness envelops him. No exit. Where is the future teller with the answer? How will this end?

Bob Nelson rubs his temples and stares at his feet, shaking his head. "This is it! If he does this . . . gets this to happen. Any of it – psychedelics, cocaine, whatever. This is it. He's lived up to his end of the bargain." He looks up for assurance and receives a couple of nods. He pushes himself up out of his chair and waits for his son to rise. There are no lectures left. No points of advice on how to create a successful life. There is only the slow trudge of going through the rest of it. The feeling of getting punched in the face every time you take a step. That is all they have left. Defeated they head out the door and leave the agents there with arms crossed over growing bellies.

Casper sits on the edge of his bed, hands and drumsticks blurring as he meticulously strikes a small practice pad that sits on his lap - growling vocals seep out of his large canned headphones.

We're gonna have a TV party tonight. All right!!!!

Drumming is currently his new obsession and this little octagon of padded silence is great practice, an imaginary snare drum. Simultaneously he paces his feet along to pretend hi-hats and a kick drum, working on his coordination. The latest music magazines cover his bed, open to the latest centerfold of cymbal porn – Zildjian. He drools over the shining gold of the finely smithed metal, envisioning the new set he'll have for his NEW LIFE in California. Far, Far away from here. Posters cover his wall, hanging from scattered mismatched thumb tacs. *Corrosion of Conformity, D.R.I., Fugazi* - Nelson called earlier and is really pushing. Everything is so damn tempting.

His mother pops her head in the door and is instantly worried about what the muffled music is doing to his hearing. He shoots her a look but restrains himself from yelling at her for barging in. She's a neurotic, fragile woman with an eggshell psyche. One wrong word from him can send her into crying hysterical fits. He's the oldest and her baby. The one she always has to worry about. Not Jacob. Jacob is smart - in a structured way. He'll do fine in the world. But Sean? Who knows where his flighty mind is? *"The kid is oblivious to any sort of reality. He thinks he's goddamn Walter Mitty."* His father would always say, making an arcane reference to some 1950's movie about a guy with an imagination so vivid he actually believes he's living out his dreams. His father had mentioned the thing so many times he finally tracked it down and watched it. Turns out it was actually a good movie starring Danny Kaye, one of the first real gay movie stars. Sean understood it was a form of communication from his father and an assurance in a way. His dad was telling him, *look there are others like you out there – someone wrote a movie about it – do something with your imagination.* Sean never knew if his dad thought these things through, but he always had a way of saying the right thing at the crucial times as though he was reading his confused mind and providing a doorway of light for him to step through.

"Dinner's ready, honey." She says it, meek as can be. Even though he does not actually hear her, he nods as though to say, he'll be there shortly. She takes that action as an answer and retreats to the world outside his room. The song takes a minute more to finish as he fleshes out the fantasy escape plans, which will come of this drug deal. He'll just need to figure out how he's going to approach and convince Waylon that he can pull this off. 100% - there can be no hint of Nelson's involvement – Waylon would slap him for even thinking about dealing with that fuckin' wastoid.

Antique trinkets everywhere accentuate the small features of the house. The faux rustic wallpaper does little to help the claustrophobic feel but does add warmth and softness. The Casper's table sits through a framed doorway outside the tiny kitchen. There's something comforting in the worn wood of the furniture. As they gather around the kitchen table, a cracked window above the sink lets a cool breeze slide through the room, tempering the heat coming from the oven. The cramped kitchen is filled with out of date appliances and looks like a scene from the 50's. The nice breeze continues softly through the doorway and around the circular pine table, big enough for only the four of them. Quaint place settings are laid out. To his mother - this is a sign of class. Clad in old-fashioned oven mitts she hustles a pan of Au Gratin cheesy potatoes from the rack to the table and lays it down on a beaded, rubber table pad.

Sean's little Brother Jacob and his father are already seated at the table. Mr. Casper has just come from his shift at the plant where he oversees the warehouse production of massive sheets of fiber insulation. The little threads of white fiber find every conceivable way in through his overalls and leave him in a constant state of itch. His eyes are continually red from the strands that sneak in through the sides of goggles and scratch at his membranes. He's ready for some comfort food and grabs it instantly as, one by one, the hot bowls hit the table – mashed potatoes, cream of corn from the can, pot roast and gravy. He adds larges amount of salt to everything and shovels in the food. Jacob lets his dad fill his plate and then takes the hand offs.

"Today in drafting I started the building I want to make someday." Jacob tells his dad.

"Did you bring it home?"

"It's not ready yet."

"Oh I can't wait to see it!" His mother chimes in with authentic, over the top excitement.

Sean enters the room with a spring to his step, his head filled with formalizing dreams. His decision made. A story hatched. He'll tell Waylon – Dave, the lifeguard they used to hang with a few years back, is the connection. He had been a few years older than them but the three had bonded over a shared love of surfing before Dave left 3 years ago to go to college in California. Sean had seen him a few times on holiday breaks and had gorged on his stories of riding point breaks along SoCal's shores. Teaching themselves to surf on Lake Erie's choppy waters, the three had braved many a winter's day together – the only time for any real waves. He laughed and marveled at the memory of themselves. There adolescent brains had only been able to acquire 3mm, ¾ quarter wetsuits, the kind with short sleeves and legs. How idiotic they had been in 50-degree water, clad in only these slabs of neoprene. In mini duck dives through the 5 foot winter waves, the first deluge of water would crash over their heads and pour down the back of their necks, filling the interior of the wetsuits with ice cold, hypothermic water. Their bodies instantly going into shock and leaving them momentarily paralyzed. Slowly, painfully, they'd bring their limbs back to life and try to paddle out through the dark, harsh gray waters - all for little 10-second rides on unreliable waves. But Dave's SoCal stories had assured him it had all been worth it.

"The real trick is getting up man. We did that a million times."

Hollywood and rock stars, skating Venice Beach, surfing Huntington and Manhattan. He saw his life in California coming true before his eyes. THE ESCAPE. Pull the cord. There's nothing here. Get out now. I'm 18 anyways. Fuck yeah, I'll do this. I'll do this deal and hell who knows, maybe even a couple more. Put away a nice little nest egg for myself and give me some time to enjoy the beaches before doing whatever it is I'm going to do. Forget anything beyond that ------------------- all that un-seeable future. Just beaches.

"What are you smiling about?" His father asks him.

"Just remembering surfing in my old wetsuit."

"Oh my gosh," His mother calls from the kitchen. "I really thought you might die."

"Get in here and eat." His father says sternly to both of them. "You finish that application to Ohio State?" Already knowing the answer.

"I read it over." Sean walks past him towards the kitchen – already gone. He grabs the phone and dials Nelson's number, excitedly tapping his fingers on the phone as it rings. Finally Nelson answers, out of breath. "You wanna come get me and talk things over? . . . Yeah. 20 minutes. Cool?" He hangs up the phone and joins his family for dinner. 30 minutes later through the lace curtains he sees Nelson's car pull up out front. The single end of a cigarette burns bright from long drags. His mother is rambling on about something and he's careful not to look out the window for too long. He needs to be out the door before she realizes he's going out with Tom Nelson. *Tom Nelson, what are you going to do with that hoodlum?* He listens for an opening, eventually becoming impatient and just pushes back from the table.

"Where are you going?" His dad says.

"Out."

"Out *where?*"

Sean looks at him as if to say, *Do we really have to have this same fake conversation every night?* "Just out. I don't know."

He's grabbing his jacket and trying to hustle out the door when THE QUESTION comes across the room.

"Who are you going out with?" His mother asks from the Kitchen.

"No one," and he's out the door. She follows his fading figure out the door and stares out the window where her worst fears are realized. Usually she's just an overprotective, helicopter parent, always blaming other people's children for her son's juvenile antics. But this time her paranoia does not do the reality that is taking shape justice. She has no idea how right her ever-present doom is.

It's midnight and I'm sneaking around back of Poppy's house, horny as all get out. I throw one small rock at the window – BAP - Jesus that was louder than I thought. Her beautiful face appears instantly and she puts up a finger telling me to hold on a minute while she makes sure her parents did not hear the noise. After a moment the window slides open. I jump on top of the air conditioner and pull myself in through the window. She's in only a long t-shirt and underwear. Instantly we're pressing our crotches against each other. She's a fantastic kisser and I cup her little firm breasts and run my hands over her little butt. Falling on the bed, she pulls my clothes off and I've already came once. No matter, I can literally do this fourteen times a night - at least that's our record. My tongue is all over her body and hers on mine. It's magic, an amazing, sizzling of skin and desire, endorphins and hormones and things we can't even comprehend - pure animal pleasure and teenage lust.

We finally take a break and collapse on the bed naked, staring at the ceiling. I tell her what the doctor said about the gunshot.

"Yeah, a .22. If it had been a inch lower it would have hit my spine ands then who knows what." I repeat the same story I've told ten times today. It's all very unreal and it'll take years for the gravity of the situation to truly dawn on me. For now I'm just a small town legend – actually shot in the projects, yahooing beer. "Grabbed one of the twelve packs, can you believe that shit?" They say. Antibiotics are helping the swelling go down and I can move my neck pretty good now.

"That is so crazy. I could have been looking at you fucking dead on the sidewalk." She punches me. "You could be a floating stream of energy right now, a little poof of nothing."

"I'm gonna have you fucking dead on the sidewalk in a minute." I say fake punching her back and she starts to wrestle with me.

"I'm gonna stick a knife in your gut and start twisting it around."

"I'll fucking rip the skin off of my face and just be a skull so you'll like me more."

"I would like you more." She laughs landing on top me, straddling and starting to grind. "My little poof of nothingness."

We press into each other as I try to comprehend the thought of death beyond the lens of Sunday school. Their grand notion of heaven and hell not meshing with the universe I see in my thoughts - Infinity inside a confined mind. Stars shine. I spin around my brain, playing movies of light, galaxies and memories, histories and futures. Timeless secrets play out from a thousand projectors, out to the end of nothingness. It's a boomerang. I'm back to earth, forever pushing to see something they say we will never see - convinced we can. I'm convinced there is no golden ceiling - no pitch-black ending - convinced it's all right here. Poppy gyrates staring straight into me, our minds our synced, seeing the NOW the same way. We've had a million existential talks over the past year; she had turned me on to a string of books that we're continually changing my life. Her eyes are black holes staring into mine. We're not locked into what they told us we were. It's warm. It's a quest we've begun. Throughout time people are passing the same message along to the secret seekers and we are on the hunt. Things are not as they seem. Come with us. A blue light. Fuck me. The current of the timeless underground sweeps us along.

"That guy shot me for 15 bucks."

Gray scaled in whites, blacks and soft grays, she's standing by the window exhaling a cigarette softly out into the night, her naked body lit by a distant moon. A young heavy soul with sunken cheekbones and eyes, the smooth curve of her hipbones all disappearing into nothingness, her features are all shadows and light. She looks sexy, gothic, ancient. Skeletal, with hair thick like a raven's feathers, she's one of Dostoevsky's fallen angels, as Kerouac would say. She is not of this place. Maybe I'm not of this place. I hope I'm not of this place.

Suddenly all serious, she turns to me, pinpointing her eyes, "Do you have any of those pills?" It takes me a moment to realize she means the Ritalin.

"Yeah, I have a few."

"Let's snort 'em."

I had never thought of doing this, but the way she says it makes it all seem very normal. "OK." I'm responding and digging through my jacket for the 4 pills I have in there. She has her hand out, reaching for them, waiting. I hand them over to her obediently. A little light flicks on over her vanity and she lays the pills out on the dresser. With the handle of a brush she starts crushing the pills into fine powder.

"Have you done this before?" I wonder aloud.

"No, but I saw some people do it at a party on the East side. Looked like they were having fun. I wanted to try it ever since."

She looks up at me with a cocked smile. What party was he at on the East side? Where was I? She is full of mysterious surprises. She has split the powder up into 2 lines and is rolling up a dollar bill.

"Come on." She motions me over to her. "You want to go first?"

I shrug, "Sure," seems like the gentlemanly thing to do. I've seen this in movies a ton of times and lean over with the dollar bill up one nostril and the other plugged with a finger. I inhale the length of the line. VRRROOOM. An instant rush through the center of my head, a tight spiral of spinning golden balls is burrowing through the top of my head and out into the air, merging me with the night. My eyes open wide and she is so clear in front of me. Poppy's eyes dive through mine. She can feel my joy and quickly bends down to take her line and join me.

We stand there staring at each other, forever bound in the moment. We are tingling, glowing - golden. I run my hands down her arms and the nerves under our skins connect and spark at each other. She shudders as a chill runs up her back and reaches out to touch my face. We are a king and queen, Egyptian, Mayan, one of the stars circling overhead, all-powerful in this floating cosmos of our own. The night pulsates. We breathe with the universe. Her hands run down my chest and we slowly move towards one another, treasuring each second of existence. For hours we stay in constant state of copulation for hours, periodically talking about the future, college and travel. I'm a year older than her, but she's on track to graduate early. I have only begun thinking of the world beyond my little town, but she has a life mapped out.

"I'm going to go Italy for a semester and then maybe Japan. I want to really dive into the whole Shinto thing. Lasso the circling thoughts of Buddhism before Buddha sat by the tree you know. I want to walk around the twisted streets of Europe, descend stairwells and slash my way through the dark crevices of distant ancient streets emerge into secret hidden parties." I just listen and my mind travels to the dark crevices – caught up in the flow - everything about her sends me on the underground current – Samadhi. The sun is coming up before we know it; her parents are rustling down the hall. Both of us are rubbed raw and sore from going at it all night. It hurts to put my underwear back on. She laughs at me as I wince and we enjoy the end of our unexpected rush of a night. I pop back out the window into the velvet morning, roll onto the dew covered grass, laughing - and turn to see her beaming smile waving at me from the window.

A week later Casper pulls his little, blue Pinto into the gravel parking lot next to the sled hill, his mind completely unaware of the potential ramifications of his actions. Only a slight instinctual notion of panic and fear deep in the back of his brain causes him to tap his fingers quickly on the steering wheel. He mistakes this instinct for excitement and tries to ride the wave of a feeling. He's too young, too sheltered, too suburban to realize what bad things can happen in an uncaring world. Six different pee-wee soccer games play out in the expanse of fields behind him. Mom and dads in their best keeping up appearances attire dot the grass. Some relax in lawn chairs and gossip about the overaggressive parents pacing the sidelines and yelling out at the field. Some care about the games, some don't. They all care what the others think of them. They stand proper.

The whole area is a plot of public land donated 200 years ago by the founder of the village with the intent that it always be a natural area. From the sled hill, past the soccer fields and through the woods are a maze of trails leading over to a sophisticated Nature Center and a Playhouse – Norman Rockwell's wet dream. A couple of kids on mountain bikes come out of the path that cuts over the ravine and carries on to the police station and pool. Casper watches them climb, turn over turn, up the incline to the top of the hill and for a moment contemplates getting out and showing them how it's done. Show them that perfect line to the two little primer jumps before needing to peddle hard and table out over the stream at the end. He's one of the only people in town that can do that, but he was always genuinely trying to show the younger kids how to pull of tricks. No, no, back to business. He'll ride his bike up here later and hit the trails.

Waylon had bought the story about supplying Dave and as he was beginning to think about expanding his operation, his interest was peaked about a potential, trusted, west coast connection. He thought this could be a major step and trusted Casper to handle this. Still, as always, he was smart about it and handed the deal over to an acquaintance of theirs - keeping himself layers removed from all transactions. There would be no connection to him. Casper looked around for Nelson's Monte Carlo. *Where was he?*

At the northern end of the parking lot sits a small gazebo-like shed sits. It has a teller window and doubles as a place to sell tickets for events like Harbor Days, - the once a year circus comes to town. Inside a federal agent crouches in its interior darkness and presses his telephoto lens up against the glass, snapping pictures of Sean Casper. Further down the road the lake bubbles with whitecaps in the distance, disappearing towards Canada. Mini-vanned, soccer moms drive past him unaware and his fingers drum along the steering wheel.

At the police station, just past the tree line behind the sled hill, Agent Ramsey is finishing wiring up Nelson. "I want you talking clear, describing exactly what you're are giving him and what you're getting in exchange. I want to hear dollar amounts and drug quantities. Ask him where it came from. How he got it. Keep it casual. Get him excited about bigger paydays to come. Take his mind off the present. You understand?"

"Yes." Nelson mumbles, his head held low.

Ramsey was tired of this place. Tired of this job. He had done his time. Having just turned 27, he needed to start living his own life instead of pretending to be someone else, especially a goddamn teenager. Maybe he'd grow a beard and people would stop thinking of him as a baby face capable of infiltrating high schools. Then he remembered he had volunteered for this role. Remembered how he felt this exact same way when it was all coming to an end in Gary High School. He smiled to himself, knowing that it was almost over. It'd be worth it in the end. Maybe he'd even get a little time off before the trial. Agent O'Riley looks on from the corner of the office. "We know this is tough Tom, but it's better than the alternative."

"Is it really?" His sarcastic response reveals a true wondering about whether or not he should have just done his time.

O'Riley does not let the thought continue. "Let's put an end to all this today." He nods decisively at Nelson who looks up through his eyelids from his downturned head, beaten.

Mushrooms and cocaine. Large bags of each sit inside Casper's glove compartment - enough to pay for a new life in California. Nelson pulls up alongside him, gets out and jumps into

Sean's passenger seat. Hidden by another line of trees, an unmarked car pulls into listening position two soccer fields away. If Casper had any inkling of something askew, he'd be put off by Nelson's mannerisms. He'd notice him looking around a bit too much and shaking nervously, notice the regret pervading his eyes. But the thought never crosses his mind, a little too much Jolt Cola the only tangent that quickly skims his consciousness. These all too familiar surroundings might as well be a womb – safe Harbor. The same soccer fields they played on together, the same sled hill, he could not feel less fearful.

"What's up man?" Nelson is reaching in his back pocket and pulling out an envelope of money. "Did you get everything?"

"Yeah, dude. I told you I would." Sean, smiles proudly, reaches over and pops open the glove compartment. "A pound of shrooms and a half fuckin' kilo of coke." He let's out a nervous giggle. "I've never even seen this shit before."

Tom's eyes pop out of his head. He is flooded with a brew of confused emotions. *Oh shit, you're going to jail for a long time – because of me. Now, finally, they will leave me a one, I will move away from here. I will disappear.*

"Dope man. I got 8 grand right here." The feds listen in, planning on how they're going to flip Casper and get him to give up his contacts. SIRENS! SPEEDING CARS KICK UP GRAVEL! MOM'S AND DADS TURN THEIR HEADS

TOWARDS THE PARKING LOT. It's TV come to life, right before their eyes. Referee's turn towards the commotion, kids stop playing. The crowd begins a slow drift over towards the scene. Two teenage boys are laid out onto the little beater car's blue hood. Handcuffs are slapped on as the feds kick their feet apart - faces press against the heat from the running engines. Tears are streaming down Casper's face. He looks at a line of little kids in too big soccer uniforms staring at him. His reality has been shattered, his mind imploding. He's going blind from the darkness. There is no future.

Descent

All the arrests had been made on graduation day, the powers that be figuring correctly that it would enable them to get the most sensational press coverage. A dozen, empty, ghost seats sticking out of the crowd with grave implications. The entire ordeal playing out on the local stage, directed by overzealous reporters constantly looking for the story that will spring them to the national theater. Chief Waters had become their star, ready to oblige at every turn, coming off like some yokel Texas sheriff or some shit, spouting off half-baked, incendiary warnings trying to scare every parent in the 42 million local suburbs about the dangers their children are facing. If it wasn't for him and his foresight in bringing the federals into the situation, who knows what would have happened in this town is the implied message.

Casper sits on the floor at the end of his bed crying the unstoppable, inconsolable cry of a child. The last remaining vestige of daylight winds through the leaves, its fingers of orange rays desperately grip the windowsill to keep from being pulled over the horizon. Outside - conjured in the sinking sun - are shaving cream fights, radar detector break-ins, pool hopping schemes and backseat dry humps - all hatched in blissful, unknowing minds. Meanwhile Sean's head swims with chaotic, tearing thoughts of cellmates, anal rape, shivs and every other damn, unimaginable thing. His brain is a vast chasm of darkness. Fucking the horror of it all.

More meagerly than ever before, his mother sticks her head in the door.

"Honey . . ." she's broken - a mouse before all of this, and now . . . dust and bones inside neurotic, eggshell skin.

"Honey," barely above a whisper. A tear runs down her cheek and seemingly emanates from her quivering voice. "It's time to go."

Music seeps from his headphones, orbits his head and Tracy Chapman's voice belies the punk rock postered scene around him.

We've got to make a decision, leave tonight or live and die this way.

Although he doesn't hear her, she believes the spastic, helpless eruption of his shaking, sobbing shoulders is the culmination of years of failed parenting and grave mistakes that have led to this day and with that, closes the door and collapses against the wall in the barely lit hallway. 10 feet apart, each of them connected to the same infinite black hole of despair, isolated in their own misery – silently wailing hysterically for their broken world.

WEB's first prosecution was under way; the Casper's sitting in the front row of the proceedings, sobbing endlessly. Evidence piled up in layers revealed the extent of the surveillance going on in our town. Picture after picture making nearly everyone complicit. Even when no charges were brought, the implications were clear and whispered through the town. They had cast a wide net, dragged dozens of students - friends - through the ringer. My parents were relieved, and amazed, that neither my brothers nor I had been implicated – legally at least. The wide-open, blank page of the future became contaminated with that heightened sense of reality – paranoia. We'd walk around looking at the trees for hidden cameras, be suspicious of every unknown car driving past. It takes root and festers, buries it way through your temples and hides in the crevices of your mind.

He had the best defense possible, John Allen, my father's best friend since grade school and local legend. A man with every possible connection in town, who had for decades made a career of taking on big cases and shooting down nearly every hotshot Ivy League attorney who came in to oppose him. They had grown up together back in the day when Cleveland was Irish versus Italians and his legal expertise had come in handy a few times for our family. But the tone was different this time. There was no talk of charges disappearing or deals being made, no talk of Irish favors was going to help the Casper's out of their nightmare. One night in my kitchen while eavesdropping on my father's conversation I hear the final line that shuttered the room into silence. "After all they've invested, they need someone to go down for this. There won't be a plea. There's nothing we can do for him."

"Jesus." I could tell by the sound of my dad's voice that it was final.

Staring into the Vacuum

I had barely escaped the bubble - a hand pressing out from the inside of a balloon. I struggle, the rubber stretching, becoming clearer - other worlds seen through the thin layer bounding me between what I know and the waiting cosmos - the force of everything trying to pull me back in, to keep me from seeing, from being. All I need is a little tear in the film to free myself forever – to be gone.

I can feel the force of her behind me, willing me to wake. My eyes open to the spikes of light seeping in through the windows. Rolling over, I see her raven hair, with streaks of dyed red strands, scattered across the pillow. Dark eyeliner frames her blue-white wolf eyes. They are wide open and staring into the black void center of me. She gives a smile and my hand runs down the smooth skin of her naked back and down to her legs. New tattoos run along her ribs and down her hips. A knife and flowers. She leans into me - a soft cocoon, a floating warmth. Poppy has changed lifetimes in 4 months I've been gone. She's wilder, heavier, on the edge of precipice, ready to roll into the universe of the night. Poppy's pupils are vast holes swallowing up everything she sees. Her limbs pilfer energy from the neurons in the air. She vibrates with life. She wants it all.

"You're beautiful in the morning." I say to her.

She gives a long cat-like stretch and smiles her half devil smile. "Oh, shut up." She purrs. "Whatcha wanna do today?" Nymph-like, she instantly pops up on the bed naked. Standing on her tiptoes, she throws her arms around the air, a gymnast wobbling on a unseen balance beam doing a playful dance. Her hair stands on end. She's all 80's hair metal rock star chick in the morning. She is simultaneously the tear in the fabric and the rubber pulling me back to what I know. Trouble is what she wants today and I'm into what she chasing. I tackle her at the knees and we tear each other apart as the bright morning blankets us.

The shower water slides down her face, washes the soap from her eyes and white foam slips down her neck and to my hands that are running up and down the smooth skin on the sides of her torso. Everything about her is beautiful; she's a glowing white light in my brain.

"Fuck, I've got to do some Christmas shopping." I've been home on break for 6 days, procrastinating as always.

"Jesus, your gonna make me go to the fucking mall on Christmas Eve aren't you?"

"Yes, you're coming with me." I kiss her, knowing she's already plotting on how to get drunk before shopping and I love her more for it. "I have about 4 more days of freedom before my parents get my first semester grades and shit themselves."

"What were you doing all fall? Cause you sure weren't calling me." She's doesn't really care and is not really scolding. She was doing her own thing anyways and just wants to put the blame on me, wants me to acknowledge that I jumped off her grid and left her alone to wallow in the depressive chasm of high school nonsense.

"I said I was sorry." I say smiling at her. "Right now is great though."

She opens her eyes from under the rush of water and stares at me with a deep understanding.

"Right now is great."

Through an arched entrance in the faux stucco wall that opens out into the mall, hundreds of shopping bags glide past our eyes in blurred festivity. At least we're not the only ones in this bad, chain, Mexican restaurant, sitting at the bar drinking at 11am on Christmas Eve. The place is a fuckin' gaggle of black sheep hiding from their families and dreading the night before them. Poppy's disdain vibrates on her face, she hates everyone and feels above them all - the leg shaking rumble of mania tickling her mind. "Doesn't everyone think that way?" She asks me.

"I know what you mean, it does no good to hate them. I mean, who the fuck are we? We're nobody's."

"Yeah," she takes a long pose, "but we know it . . . that makes
It different."

"That definitely makes it different, but . . . " I need to think
about it . . . The kind bud we puffed making each moment a
realization, the flood of words runs through my mind like an out of
control computer. Philosophy 101 classes are skipping through my
brain – the examined life - I'm sailing past Nietzsche's nihilism
and am full fledged on the light – spiraling - I've taken
Kierkegaard's fucking leap man. I BELIEVE. If it's all madness,
death and godlessness, what's the harm in believing? Now I'm
wrapped in the energy of the universe. I get vague glimpses of
Buddha and know I want to know more, I feel connected to the
lights tunneling through the air. I see myself with a gray beard on a
green rolling hill, I must be in my eighties. The sun is shining on
my face and I'm at peace. That's who I will be.

"Yeah. It does make us different." I agree and she's happy
about it. Nodding in intellectual conquest, she takes a gulp of her
whiskey and let's out a loud exhale. "All right, let's go get your
fuckin' family some shit."

She's skipping through the mall, her mere presence mocking
everyone around her. She relishes in it, antagonizes strangers,
LIVES like they don't live.

"So what the fuck?" She laughs at me. "Are you going back again after break?"

"Yeah? What the hell else am I going to do?"

"Anything! You can do anything." She means it.

I shake my head at her, but she sees through it.

"I'm serious." She says laughing. "You got any money?"

"No."

She skips up onto the brick ledge wall of a wishing well waterfall. "Well shit. Get a job for a few months, save some cash. I'm graduating early. Let's go to Europe or Asia or some islands, pet some monkeys." Balancing on her tip-toes, she throws her arms around merrily. "Ahhhhhh!!!!!!" She yells. The whiskey kicking in. "I wanna pet some monkeys!!!!!!"

She's infectious, a boa constrictor, her sinewy energy twines around me. I want to explode with her, blow the whole fucking thing up, burst into a ball of light and spin off into the universe. I grab her by the legs and whip her over my back and start running her through the mall as she play spanks my ass.

"Let's go get fucked up!" I say as she bounces on my shoulder.

It's a quick drive downtown to Waylon's place. He's moved into a nearly empty building overlooking 6th street – the beating, cocaine heart of the city. Hardly anyone lives down here, so it's a ghost town during the day. The clubs that line the street are shuttered with metal gates, waiting for the sun to set and the vampires to come play. With no one to pan handle from, homeless people don't even venture here. We pull up and park right out in front of his building, the only car on the street.

As we enter the front door, the gears of a camera's motor crank, turning its eye to stare down at us from the corner of the ceiling. I give it a smile, the door buzzes and we glide through the glass doors. Apart from the grey carpet, everything is white – the doors, the hallways, the lights. Even though the place has been open a year, it still smells of fresh paint and new construction from the lack of tenants. Waylon lives on the top floor, all the way in the back of the building with a view of downtown and Lake Erie. I give a rap on his door and we enter into the sterile, antiseptic smell of cocaine.

Poppy has never been here before and I instantly regret bringing her. Her eyes bulge from her head as she takes in the motley crew of derelict apparitions floating through the place. Waylon's little harem of barely clothed, beach blonde coke whores walk by, all tight assed with perfectly doctored breasts preparing them for their future lives of pole dancing. An old girlfriend of mine from high school is sitting in the corner of the kitchen catatonically staring straight ahead. Her eyes are tight tunnels spiraling through the now, past us, through walls and she is enthralled at something beyond. A quido-looking dude known as "The dentist" splays fat and sloppy on the couch, his stomach bulging through his black and grey striped, silk shirt. The Dentist apparently still has a practice somewhere, but never seems to leave that couch and is obviously blowing through all of his money. He is such a constant mess no one is sure he ever speaks actual words, just stammering incoherently non-stop and punctuating the mumbles with periodic nods as if emphasizing some well phrased point. The camera from the front door plays on a TV behind him. The surveillance footage brings a hyper reality to the illegality of the place.

Our buddy, Hayden, sits on the living room floor, slicing up massive lines on the glass coffee table for him and a newfound friend. It's two in the afternoon and they are eagerly trying to outdo each other with the size of the mounds they are snorting. I can't tell if it's a wake up or a stay awake session. Hayden has become a dreadlocked scenester and the local DJ du jour. He lives here with Waylon. Although at 20, the pair of them are technically too young to be in the bars, they are the kings of the scene regardless, controlling the night from the VIP sections of every club in town, appearing from nowhere and now knowing everyone there is to know. Hayden's affable manner makes him liked by all and enables a thousand smooth handshakes and meeting of the drug minds. In between hacking coughs from the powder sneaking it's way into their throats, he and his newfound friend share a two days binge worth of inside jokes.

"This is what God feels like." The friend says laughing, as Hayden turns up at him wide-eyed. In the flash of that moment, I realize it's a stay awake session and who knows when they last slept. The Dentist stares on drooling, wanting a little taste of God himself. "I am smaller than everything," the friend continues with a chuckle of disbelief. "I have left the grid."

Hayden nods knowingly, "This is where I'm supposed to be. Right?" He pauses for an answer, but then answers himself, nodding. "Yeah. Yeah. Yeah. I can feel the vibration. Feel that? Low?" The friend slows himself and nods. He feels it as well.

I don't know what else they've been doing, but knowing Hayden there were mushrooms involved. Poppy is staring at them longingly. She wants in now and turns to me wild-eyed. Her future plays across her eyes. She's staring out into the vacuum of it all. She won't escape. I see bad trouble for her. I'm channeling through time and know I should walk her out off there NOW, but I too want to feel the vibration of the giant breath of the universe. I give her a look and let the final thought of me doing the right thing dissipate. I nod at her knowingly and turn to go find Waylon – telepathically she follows.

We walk down the hallway as more waif-like girls float past, coming from Waylon's room, beautiful with dark circles for eyes.

They walk on tip-toes and rub their noses feeling like part of some 80's glamour movie in Miami. They are in the know, in the empty void womb circle where it's dark and warm, they are the scene. Waiting for Godot, never knowing what's out on the edge. Each one thinks they are it and pay no heed to the tingle of anxiety and fear forming in the galaxies beyond their grasp. The chemicals rush up the backs of their necks, icy electricity. Waylon is plying them with coca and soon they'll do anything to keep it coming. It's the same for everyone here. He has his pick of the litter, giving 'em a little teat to suckle. Soon they won't feel so special. He'll need them to do favors for him. They are slowly becoming slaves to forces they only vaguely sense exist.

Inside the room, Waylon sits on the bed with the two prettiest girls next to him, fawning – stars of the now. There is a cereal bowl full of cocaine on a black trunk in front of them. Residue dusts the spaces between lines. Watching over his concubines Waylon plots and enjoys with a suspicious mind. He wants a clear mind to take over the downtown business and so doesn't use – yet. It's amazing how clearly he can see it all, how small and simple it appears to him. Club by club, connection by connection, there are no mysteries for him. Except for Finn, Hayden and I, he doesn't trust anyone. It had been a close call with Casper and the feds had done everything in their power to get to him. For a minute the mountain of evidence presented seemed overwhelming, but by some miracle he made it out clean. A FREE MAN. Still the gravity of the game, he was in, was not lost on him. He was keenly aware of the enemy. He was constructing a new version of himself, bulletproof and stealth. He knew there were eyes everywhere. He lived in complete awareness, paranoia being his ultimate form of reality. This was his living; there were no other choices for his future. He became a warrior and now his empire was coming together. He had it all. The cars, the girls, the drugs and the endgame was just more of the same.

He turns to see us. "Hunter! Poppy! Merry fuckin' Christmas!" Trusted faces being the most fabulous thing in the world to him, he bounces up, steps across the bed and gives us each a hug. "Whatcha doin' down here?"

"We came to see you."

"Well great. What can I get you?" There's no pretense. He assumes we want something and is all smiles about it.

"Couple bumps?" I shrug my shoulders. I have never tried coke and barely even know what I'm talking about, but it's magnetic pull has been calling from distant, endless, dark rivers, from books and songs, from traditions passed down throughout time. Waylon laughs a hearty laugh that causes everyone to turn and look at him admiringly. "A couple bumps, yeah right. Come on sit down, take what you like." He kicks the two model types off the bed. "Couple of bumps he says". He laughs at me and uses a credit card to scoop out a pile of fluffy Peruvian flake onto the chest and hands me a rolled up dollar bill. I glance at him, take it and snort the little mound. It's soft and comforting inside my nose. I swallow the residue that went down my throat at the same time the rest hits my brain and I feel the magic.

I think of ceremonies and rituals and plants and medicine. It feels so natural and right to be powerful. I mimic things I've seen, run my finger over the leftovers and rub it on my gums. My mouth goes numb. I breathe in the scene around me and see Poppy's beauty, every inch of her. She grabs the dollar bill and leans in herself.

The energy is radiating through my veins, my muscles tighten - instant invincibility, smooth and flowing. My brain sizzles as thousand books rise to the surface, a million articles, myriad ancient passages. I have endless recall. I can discuss anything. This is the fucking leap. This is the fucking leap. I've made it through the center of the sun and am turning to look back on it all. Portal after portal, all the lies they told us of these things. I'm bouncing from light to light, bliss to bliss, spirits float up from the mist to steer the boat and grant my wish. I am shaman. I am poet. I am a club king ready to dance with firm hookers through the night.

Three hours later we walk out into the late afternoon sun, bite marks in our necks, immortality in our veins. We've grown fangs and the light is pain. I turn to look at Poppy and her pupils are massive. She is all-knowing, all-seeing, the knowledge of centuries evaporating inside a lonely condo in the middle of nowhere. We time travel back to the burbs. We levitate - are controlled, swept along by the sunshine rays of fate, strands of pre-destined motion. This has all been decided before us, before you . . . before. The evening passes like a golden explosion in the Midwest winter – a beautiful white heaven hanging over us. We were at the top of our games, bastions of information. The mounds of blow, Waylon supplied as a parting gift, were laid out on center consoles between the houses of our respective families. Periodic trips to the bathrooms maintained our energy throughout the night. Relatives swished hastily about the rooms ornamented with tray upon tray of homemade delicacies. The smiles only families and sages can know. My grandfather, ornate in pew going clothes, staring at me, deaf and speechless, communicating all the same, slashed away the turmoil in my mind. My rosary knelt grandmother, merciless with her smile. Everyone so thoroughly impressed with our academic achievements and our ability to drink cases of beer and never slur a word. We floated above them all. It was our own little movie as we caught each other's eyes sideways across the rooms – knowing. We were creating a new world on a new frontier, our machetes slashing through the night, slicing vortexes into the air. We were wading in the river, everyone so unaware. It was that first time.

The one you always hear about and always work to get back. Poppy and I rode our rocket ship straight into the burning star galaxies. We were ancient time travelers, our fates entwined. We'd been here before, owned the universe, were part of it for the first time.

We said our goodbyes and walked out the wreath-encircled front door, out into the tree lined front yards, dusted with snow, our laughter winding through the knotted trees, wanting to be filled with everything more. The evergreen of Christmas Eve lingering outside the house, lodging the innocence of a first snow, emerald hands peering sporadically through the timeless, ivory blanket for a final winter's glimpse at the diamonds in the sky. The fire shooting from our fingertips mingled with the neurons in the air. We relished our deep breaths of omniscience.

9pm. How could that be? I was born this morning, died at dusk. Lifetimes are a funny thing. I'm on autopilot, heading in a vague direction.

"You wanna go to the lake?" I ask her.

She turns to me dazed, slack jawed, the energy has drained from her face. She nods at me with a distant amazement, the faint hint of a smile at the corner of her mouth. She is beautiful. She's in her own place right now, finding something, but nods in response to my lake question.

"You wanna line? We got a little left."

She just shakes her head at me and I chuckle.

"O.K. little one. Let me know if you need something."

We park by her parent's house, a few of blocks of tree-lined streets from the beach. Holding hands, we make our way down the undulating sidewalks, across Lake Road and over to the dirt and gravel path that leads from there down the hill to a little cove. The path was formed centuries ago by a stream and then treaded by animals until we came to smoke cigarettes and ponder the future, live in the now or get lost in memories. The incline down to the water parallels another frozen stream that leads to a miniature waterfall in the summer, but has turned to a few translucent icicles. In a flash of a moment, they hold all of the answers to the universe. We might as well be in Antarctica as we stare out at the frozen drift of Lake Erie shoreline, stretching white towards the horizon, where everything melds into a foggy grey. The cold doesn't seem to touch me, only lilting around my exposed skin, reminding me of life. Our love has become something it never was before. She is Cleopatra, I am Caesar, I am Rimbaud, she's my Nubian princess. We have lived eons together, been a million things. I throw my arms out at the expanse and ramble.

"We are in the forever loop of rebirth, this mad illusional, delusional déjà vu of reality testing our resolve. But we know it's good to be here. Right?" She doesn't answer. "Right? It's good to be in the absurdity of it all. The stars are so close, I feel like we're laughing in God's face!" I turn to her covered in my own astonishment at the truth of it, "I really want to know it all, you know?" I say. She sits there listening to me talk, not hearing a word I'm saying. She's off floating in the swirling chaotic universe at the back of her own brain. She's discovering versions of herself she never knew existed. We don't dream of 30 years from now, we dream of now. We will die soon in a fiery explosion of imminence. It's the only logical conclusion. Humans cannot continually exist feeling this good. She's becoming confused and spinning. The cold air is not reviving her as it does me, Everything she ever thought to be real is cracking before her, inside her. I am inside my own vortex and do not notice. My arms are outstretched as I inhale deeply, filling my lungs and pumping my chest. My muscles flex. Dopamine shoots up my neck. I am energy. My aura is seeping out of my skin and electrical charges coming out of my head. The universe invades until there is no delineation between the night sky and us. I do not even know what I'm saying any longer as a million tangents lead me down rivers of thought from which I cannot find my way back upstream to my point.

"Like Godard said, I don't digress, I enter a big subject." I say to her, laughing, knowing I've lost my way.

"I can't stay here." Poppy whimpers. I turn to see she has slid down to the ground. I smile at her, but she's not amused and I see it's time to go. "Oh cutie. Why didn't you say something?" I reach down to help her up, her dead weight making me instantly realize it's going to be a long walk back. I let her sit for a minute and pull my keys from my pocket, dip it into my little folded up paper of powder and take a bump to gather strength - an old pro now. I'm gonna go fucking conquer the world, I think as I throw her over my shoulder. Everyone will see.

The trek up the hill with her takes everything I have out of my legs. She is sleeping now and there's no waking her. I stare down the long road that was such a pleasant walk only an hour before. In the distance I can see the neon lights, of the small convenience store, sneaking through the bare winter limbs. I instantly feel like a dirtbag bastard as I make my plan. Turning towards some brush alongside the rocky path, I carry Poppy that way and lay her down a couple of feet in. Pulling some branches over her, I glance back towards the neon lights and think this is the only way. Taking a deep breath, I set out at a good clip, running down the street. I'm a bit too fast out of the gate and only a half a block away I'm walking, out of breath. I gather strength and trot into a slower jog, but the day's festivities are wreaking havoc on my cardio and I stop again not shortly after. I repeat this process a half dozen times until I'm alongside the store, hands on my knees, heaving. A half a dozen shopping carts sit next to the dumpsters and I check them for crappy wheels and find one I like. Leaning back for a second against the brick wall, I collect myself and make my way back.

Now that I have someone else's property, the road one over from the main street will give me more cover. I head that way and halfway down the block when headlights appear from Lake Road, heading towards me. Arrows of light are shooting at me between the hedges. I leave the shopping cart on the sidewalk and make my way tree by tree through a front yard. Not wanting to lose my last bit of coke and needing a place to hide, I sneak alongside a small little cottage. Lights pop on as I set off motion sensors on two houses. Lit up as though I just stepped on stage, I spring into the darkness of the backyards and look out towards the street. Sure as shit, it's a cop and he's shining his spotlight on the shopping cart. The metal bouncing little yellow beams of light around it's cage. I hear his radio crackle something and can't believe my luck right now. I pull the coke out of my pocket ready to ditch it in the snow. The lights on the houses flick off one after another and the cop's light bounces around the wooden siding. PISS!!! I remember my footprints just as his spotlight finds them between the houses. I take off through the yards behind me, knowing I need to make it to the shoveled sidewalk. I hear the car start to back up and dodge the spotlight like I'm in fuckin' Compton or something. I make it to the sidewalk back on the main street and sail across the tree lawn onto the asphalt road. Adrenaline pumping, I sprint up a driveway,

128

sail across someone's front walk, up to their porch. Hiding behind a couple of empty plant pots I'm thankful that I've not ditched my stash yet and wait. But then I see another cruiser coming from the direction of the convenience store. Of course, what the hell else are they going to be doing tonight? The cop flicks its spotlight on my side of the street and creeps past me at a crawl. I duck as the light washes over me and realize I must have a couple of the belly over the belt old boys out tonight. No way they are getting out of their cars and slogging through the snow to chase a shopping cart thief. I'll just have to wait them out a bit longer – and then I think of Poppy.

I have blood coursing through me like a maniac, but the frost is seeping into my toes and fingers now. I don't know if sleeping is helping or hurting her in the cold right now. I curse these police and their lack of anything better to do. They are now a couple of streets away, circling, waiting me out. They know it's cold out here and if they can't flush me out, they at least want to inflict some pain. I decide I need to risk it and check on her. The last remnants of crushed white powder are only a small tease as they line my nose and I lick the paper clean. In a flash I'm on the sidewalk, pushing aside my dozen beers and depleted serotonin. The trees are sketching snakes from the earth as I watch the lights scatter through the trees and I'm crossing back over Lake Road before I know it. Crouching, I make way to her and can hear her breathing over the snapping twigs. Her nose is ice cold and her fingers look blue, but it could be the night-light mixing with my guilt and paranoia. I sit in the brush and bring her onto my lap. I rub her back and watch the streets. I hold her so tight and she warms me. I say I'm sorry a thousand times. Sorry for the whole thing. I remember my moment of decision when we should have left Waylon's earlier in the day. I pull her tighter.

After another 15 minutes everything is quiet. The lights are gone.

"Poppy. Come on, can you get up? Poppy!"

Nothing. I kiss her forehead and run.

The shopping cart sits where left it, a shining booby trap lying in wait. I have no time to think it though and I'm instantaneously flying down the center of the street, pushing the cart in a parallel universe past shining Christmas lights and parents sneaking downstairs to lay presents under the trees. The single streetlamp above the beach entrance lights my scene again as I cross Lake Road. The last surge of adrenaline helps me lift Poppy into the cart and then I'm drained, with nothing left. I will leave it up to fate at this point and start my slow walk, down the center of streets, back to her parent's place, resigned to whatever I encounter as her slow breaths rise from her mouth like chimney smoke into a soft fog.

The house sits shrouded in shadows, vague gray lines and skull like black holes disappearing into emptiness. The silence is intimidating as I push her up the slight incline of the driveway, trying to minimize the squeaking of the wheels, only hoping I can find an open door to slide her into. She has not moved on the 15-minute walk and I know she will not wake as I turn her onto the path in front of her porch. I place a rock behind a wheel to keep her from rolling back down the driveway and begin searching her. There are no keys in her pockets or purse so my first hopes of ease are dashed. Cold wind whispers past my ears, the night is heavy on me as I creep up to the front door and creak open the storm door, each millimeter of opening sending a new staccato shriek into the darkness. The knob does not turn - another hope dashed. I check each first floor window – nothing. It's getting cold and my hands are numb. The swallow of a winter night is pulling us in. I need the ice to evaporate, climb into the night, converge upon a thought and form the summer sun.

I'm gonna have to pop a screen and hope to get an open window. I figure the dining room on the right side of the house is the furthest from her parent's room, so I go there first. I bend the thin metal. CRACK. The sound reverberates. I push it a little more to take it from its hinges and start to slide it up just as the . . . FLASH, the light inside flicks on. "FUCK. FUCK. FUCK". I say under my breath. Around the corner I can see Poppy's sad puppet limps hanging marionette like over the sides of her metal cage. The front porch lights flick on and illuminate her sorry state. There's nothing I can do but run. The front door opens as I make it to the next yard.

"Jesus Christ. What the . . . ?" Distraught, Poppy's father goes to grab his frozen daughter. Lifting her up like the little baby she is to him, he scans the streets with hate. Someone will die. I imagine the scene of her lying on the foyer carpet as he rubs her warm, his fiery brain imaging everything to be a million times worse than it is.

My feet are soaking wet as I walk through the back yards. I can feel my muscles constricting against my ribs as the wind drives deep and shivers its way to the marrow of my bones. Buzz gone, I am just staring into sober reality, my heart pumps heavy against my sternum, tinges of despair are circling. Golden strings of Christmas lights shine warm everywhere making me feel separate from all there is. I should go home and limit the night's damage, but the demons need to be quelled - or given their just due. I don't know which, but I have to find out. The ground beneath me opens up as I head to the bar to find Finn.

Jimmy's is way beyond capacity and five bartenders hustle to fill the empty hands. Arms slung around each other's shoulders, rock and roll versions of Christmas tunes are bellowed from reunited friends swaying back and forth on the barroom floor. The doorman sits slumped at the entrance and apathetically takes my ID. He gives me a suspicious look from the corner of his eye, but nods his head, telling me to pass. It's a mishmash of people at this annual holiday high school reunion. There's people 5 years older than me milling about, post college, busy pretending as though they are worldly now, Slightly older people stand awkwardly and put on airs of success and beyond that the sad eyes of people desperately wondering where real happiness lies. My reptilian brain is thankful to see Waylon has ventured out to the burbs and sits at a booth, holding court, with a small harem. Flocks of degenerates circle his vicinity, all angling to score. Finn buzzes about the room belly laughing with everyone there.

"Hey fucker." Finn sees me and slides his way through the crowd to give me a hug. He looks me up and down. "Jesus. Where you been?"

"Man. You would not believe my last couple of hours. I need a fuckin beer bad."

"Well get one then dipshit." He slaps me on my back and I slog my cold bones over to the bar and make eyes with a girl I know serving drinks. She sees me through the swarm and I mouth "VODKA" with only mildly feigned desperation.

She nods with a smile and does a quick, large pour. "First is on me." She says as our arms reach through the layers of people and I throw a five on the bar for a tip and turn back towards the throngs as the liquid warms me. I push through a dense, mist version of reality, my world going foggy. I'm laughing and hugging, spinning tales of my successful first year at school and my future Machiavellian plans to take over the world. Finn makes faces behind me telling people not to believe a word I say. Waylon sneaks me another little pouch of powder. I'm on autopilot, riding ups and downs, alternately sailing above the crowds and sinking into molasses. Jukeboxes blur past my eyes. It's a carnival of jesters and circus freaks, heads and shoulders and vague faces. People's names failing me, speech failing me. Nod and smile. Feel good. Move forward. Hazy. Wide-eyed. This is my new adult life. People are fucked, sloppy, especially this girl. She is so fucked up. What is she on? Her face is drooping off of her skull. Avoid that guy in the rugby. He's a cop, has to be. Why is he looking at me? Paranoia dances with invincibility. It's too bright, the bartenders are telling everyone to leave. I am disembodied, numb, a floating mind. I'm falling towards a table. I'm laying in a hospital bed, blood streaming out of my eye. The world is cycling around me. The night is a blur. I'm desperately trying to keep from passing out as I wait for the doctor. There's a TV on in front of me that I can't focus on. It's a blue blur whose sound dissipates into it's own outer atmosphere allowing me to tune into hear the happenings in the bed next to me. Finn is outside my room being asked to leave the premises. There's a girl who has come into the hospital in severe pain from constipation and she's getting an enema. Am I really here? They have a curtain pulled around her and her parents are consoling her that all will be right. I am fascinated with my reality.

The doctor arrives and looks at me with hate. He's just kicked Finn out after finding him passed out on the waiting room floor. There goes my ride. Apparently I have a chunk of wood in my eye from falling onto the corner of a table. "It's a small miracle I'm not blind right now". The doctor looks at it, grabs some forceps or some such contraption and begins pulling. From my other eye I can see past the tip of my nose as my skin stretches until the piece finally pops out. He drops it in a container, shaking his head with disgust at my drunken state and quickly begins, haphazardly, putting in stitches that will certainly leave the biggest scars he can. I'm fading in and out, the room is going black – I can hear the girl next to me squirming and whining through her ordeal. I need to get up before I throw up all over myself.

"You're all done," the doctor tells me with disdain. I gingerly push myself up from the bed as he begins to realize the full extent of my impairment, but not soon enough. I hit my feet, lose my balance and immediately begin stumbling across the room, by arms flailing like some crazed person falling from a building. He reaches for me but misses and I crash through the pale blue curtain pulled around the bed next to me - landing on top of the ENEMA GIRL.

"Ahhhhhhhhhhhhh!!!!!" She screams a guttural scream that will live with me for the rest of my life. She has no idea what has just happened. Has the room caved in on her? Is she being attacked? I laugh inside my spiraling mind. The doctor reaches me in a flash, and grabbing the back of my shirt, whips me back towards my bed as the girls parents pull the curtain off their newly blanketed daughter.

"Jesus Christ." They all scream in unison. The daughter pops up gasping, her bulging eyes joining all the others staring into the sad sack that I am.

"Get me a wheelchair in here." The doctor yells into the hall as he goes over to the family. "I am so sorry about this." He asks tenderly, "Is everything still in place?"

This is not happening. A laugh wells up from deep inside of me forcing my body to shake. My shoulders start to shudder as I try not to puke. Just as a nurse pushes the chair in, I begin projectile vomiting across the room directly at her. I am laughing hysterically now as a green geyser shoots from my mouth, her face dropping as though she's watching The Exorcist only amplifies my laughter. I clean my system and become remarkably lucid.

"Get him out of here." The doctor screams to the nurse.

Thrown in a wheelchair, I'm rolled outside the hospital. If the staff could get away with beating me, they would. Instead, they just blow their lips in disgust, turn away and leave me to the night. The cold black air grips my face and I again can see neurons creating pathways through the air, it's a rush of undeniable, vivid energy. I replay the hilarity of the scene I just created inside the dome theater of my brain and laugh to myself. After a moment, I stand up and go to the payphone by the entrance to call Poppy. When her dad answers, my voice fails me.

"Hello." He says, his voice searching for my identity. "Hello? Hunter if this is you, you'd better hope to God I don't ever see you again."

I hang up - shattered. Just as the universe solidified our love, it throws up a burning wall. Did she wake up and talk? No way. How much does he know? Why would she tell him? What did she tell him? I'm despondent, pulled into a forever abyss of hopelessness as I hang up the payphone and catch a glimpse of my reflection in the glass of the hospital entrance. My face mixes with scattered lights coming from all directions, distorting my image. I am frozen, staring at someone I do not know – a tear in the fabric. I recognize a strangeness in me. Something I like. There's a soundless communication with time. The stars behind me form a celestial halo as though I'm floating between worlds. My reflection moves separately from me. I stare at my other self fully for the first time, noticing the odd sensation of being in two places at once. An exchanged wink acknowledges that nothing is really real. Do what you want with this life. There is no course. A coldness washes over my heart. We cannot pretend to know. My aura is seeping out of my skin, a white yellow force field, my electrical charges combining with those snaking through the air. I stare deeply into myself, trying to unite me. Unable to pull myself together, I leave a version of myself in the window as my reflection turns and walks away into the night.

Having pushed presents aside to make room for myself after the five mile walk from the hospital, my parents find me beneath the Christmas tree. The stairs must have been too daunting at six this morning. I'm growling from the lack of sleep as they try to wake me. Doorbells are ringing. I hear the sound of children - my small cousins climbing over me. They think I'm playing. My father leans down to my ear.

"Goddammit Hunter. You'd better get up right now." I know I must and make a painful turn to face everyone.

"Jesus!" He and my mother exclaim simultaneously. I grunt and remember the hack job of stitches under my eye. "What happened to you?" My mother instantly convinced I was beaten and left under the tree by a gang of hooligans – obviously.

"Long story." I grumble, the pain in my head making it impossible to stand up. I crawl on all fours towards the stairs, thinking I can get out of sight and disappear back into sleep.

"Do not even think about it." My father admonishes. "You better be back down here in 10 minutes." It does not seem possible. There is zero likelihood of that happening. I am sick like I've never been sick before. A vice pulsates on my temples, crushing my skull into my sinuses. My heart races, skips beats and flutters on top of my flipping stomach, pumps toxins out to my shaking limbs and yet I do not have a choice. Surely the world will end. On my knees, hanging over the toilet and dry-heaving, I reach into my pocket with a ray of hope and find what I'm after. There's enough for a bump up each nostril. It blows my eyes open, clears the room in a concentrated explosion of NOW. Clarity returns. I splash water on my face and look at the jagged stiches poking from beneath my eye. *Yes. Let's go do this day.*

In between unfurling wrapping paper, squealing children and platters of desert trays, I try Poppy every 30 minutes, lapsing into the universal teenage code -calling and hanging up after one ring. Finally she calls me back at 8 that night. I pick up on the first half ring.

"Hello?"

"You have to stop calling here. My parent's know it's you."

"Well, why didn't you call me back then?"

"Why didn't I call you back?" She sounds indignant. It does not occur to me that's she's angry.

"Yeah."

"Umm, cause you left me in a shopping cart in the middle of the night to freeze to death."

"You passed out, I was trying . . ." A click on the line.

"Poppy? Who are you talking to?" The sound of her father's voice sends me into hiding. I shrivel back into my hole. No explanation will ever make it right for him.

"I was just telling Hunter to stop calling."

I can't believe what I'm hearing. I lean back against a wall. My insides are being ripped out of my body. She's literally prying my ribs open with a crowbar and exposing the cavity of my black, fucking black misery. I can hear her father take a deep breath and restrain himself from tearing into me. "One more minute." He says and hangs up.

"Poppy." I plead. "You passed out. What was I supposed to do?"

"I don't know. Knock on the door?" She says sarcastically.

"I was trying to get into the house when you're dad came out." She's not hearing me.

"It doesn't matter. I'm not allowed to talk to you anyways."

I slide down the wall, hitting the ground with a defeated thud, collapsing inside myself, dreaming of knives through my eyeballs. A star smolders in the distant night.

I'm back at school with the lure of a parallel world continually hovering around me, a magnetic pull to a dark center not far away, leaving this place to feel so plastic and hollow. I sit in classrooms thinking of madness and questioning the soul, periodically snapping out of my fugue state to argue with professors about altruism and relativism, empiricism and rationalism. Despising my questions and my existence they stare at the thermos they rightly suspect is filled with vodka. They want to shove it down my throat along with their pre-determined notions. All the while I'm being metaphysically dragged back by the call of the scene, the underground seduction that does not exist in the manicured lawns and classrooms locked inside the hundred year old buildings of America. The generic frat parties crowded with solo cups and upside down beer stands become transparently juvenile. People are stunted in time. I find myself creeping out of side doors and out into the night to make the drive downtown. More and more I make the drive.

Speeding past the violet flames of the factories billowing clouds of toxic waste and the green blue film on the river.

Smokestacks, with their pungent smells, cough into the air filling the surrounding mobile homes of workers doing all and anything they can to make it in the world. Burning lungs and twisting chromosomes. Riding a roller coaster of despair, I think of Poppy. The embryonic, fetal thoughts of a possible future with her had taken me to the sunlit pinnacle and now due to the impossibility of it all, I'm falling fast. The shadows dance. I wonder what she is doing right now. The thought of her takes me to the sea, a warm breeze lifting over the dunes. Soon I will ride high, conqueror again. Cocaine bliss is coming my way. I am almost there. The lights of the city dazzle me. A change of air is what I need. It's a good thing to suffer Dostoevsky told us - fling yourself straight into life without deliberation - he ended up in jail.

Winding through the cosmos as pure thought I float through parties where hours of nonsensical conversations cure the universe, - nothing ever mattering except that we were once alive and free to do whatever we wanted. I am unafraid to take the starry leap into infinity. AK-47's. Backstages. Opium in shampoo bottles, smuggled from Holland. Local celebrities drift by my eyes. Undercover police. There's a conspiracy. The bars serve water laced with MDMA. Everyone grinds their teeth and dances. Massive speaker cabinets pound bass lines through chest cavities, move closer. Nine Inch Nails "Something I Can Never Have" creates it's world, reflects mine. Porn plays on a thousand screens.

Images flash, the line between television waves and brain disappears. Alleyways twist and lead to doorways, deeper into the night. Pounding. Dance. Twirl. Grind. There's an answer here somewhere. The nights swept along in broken sight, I walk past secret rooms, curtains pulled to hide beautiful girls with needles it their arms. Maniacal laughter echoes down vandalized hallways. More doorways. People plan convenience store robberies. I follow a distant blue light squirming out of site. Tunneling, I'm driving back home blinded by the rising sun, surrounded by myriad morning commuters. My mind is drifting through the top of my head, squinting my eyes, trying to pull focus. The steering wheel separates into three different versions in front of me and I'm losing grip of it somehow, the cars around me start to slide by the window in blurred lines of metal and grass. The wheel rips from my hands as I try to pull it back to center. I'm going down. Pull the throttle up. My arms shake with the violence of it. Tires skid sideways across the grass. The car leans and throws me into the door and then whips me back over the center console as it all comes to an amazing silence. I'm frozen in the median staring at the bloodstream of traffic on both sides of me. Heart it races. A thousand distorted faces slow to look at me. Everything remarkably clear, I gun the gas, ripping back onto the road, an autopilot space traveler at warp speed towards comfort and safety. Collapsing onto bed, the world spins.

I awake weeks later, shaking. Slowly, painfully re-entering the world from another time. The crisp light hurts my eyes and stings my skin. The reality of a new day - a real world pounding at the door. Flipping my legs over the side of the bed, my cigarettes are just within reach and I try to inhale away the questions. A month of missed classes having left me in a predicament. Professors that hated me before will not be willing to cut me any slack. I don't know what to do so I call Finn and he answers groggily.

"What's up man?"

"Dude, I'm about to get kicked out of school"

"Whaddya do?"

"Nothing, I've just been hanging out at Waylon's, not going to classes."

"That'll do it. Whatcha gonna do?"

"I have no idea." There's silence on the line as he empathically shares my fate.

"Man, my roommate had mono for like six weeks and they let him take all his exams. I don't think he ever even gave 'em doctor's notes or nothing."

"Yeah?" A vague sense of hope washes over me. There's always a reason to consult with Finn. "Fuck it. Sounds like a plan."

"Let me know how it goes." He says happy with himself and hangs up.

Hell, I must look sick. I'll tell them one by one that I have mono. It's the only solution. Some of them might not buy it and I'll just take the "F's" and hope the rest evens out my grade point. "Deadly ill," I say, "Unable to get out of bed. Just let me take the exams." I'll cram. I'll pass. I'll get past this, onto something. The next thing. The new thing, whatever it is. Dr. Harris is chasing me down the hall.

"Get the hell out of here, you pompous fool."

Fuck him. Fuck statistics. Fuck college. I move faster away through the tiled echoes, a void of 1890's architecture.

"You will go nowhere in this life!" his vitriol a winding dragon chasing me out of the building. That's what he wants for me - to go nowhere. To die a miserable death because he despises everything I am and anyone like me. Plan B. What is plan B? There's always a plan B.

"What are you doing home?" My mother is surprised to see me as she walks in the door with bags full of groceries. The classic kitchen feels easy, light. Pantries and stainless steel, handcrafted woodwork meld seamlessly together. Her presence confirms the sanctuary, safety from the encroaching world. The twisted manacles lurking just out of sight from everyone else can't reach me here.

"I just thought I'd say hi and get a little home cooked meal."
The mail has not yet arrived. I've checked three times now, but
fully expect my grades to be coming today. If I can pull this off,
they won't know I've been kicked out of school for another couple
of months. A successful day means the party keeps going. By then
I'll figure something out.

"You hate my cooking." She says as she places the brown
plastic bags on the counter. The window above the kitchen sink
paints soft lines of light across her, mixing in dark stokes from the
shadow of leaves. She looks at me quizzically, focusing on my
eyes which are likely sunken and red. "You feeling ok?"

"I like some things you make." I say dodging her question.
"Can you make that chicken stuffing, cheese thing?"

"Yeah, I think I have the ingredients to make it." She's pulling
items out of the bag and wondering what's becoming of her eldest
son. I can feel her looking for a way in. An inquiry into my current
affairs is simmering. Clouds blot out the sunbeams and the window
goes dark for a moment. I catch a confused potion of wonder and
concern crinkling her brow. I can feel the tension build, the
manacles leaching their way into the sanctuary and I want to avoid
the conversation.

"Sweet. I'm gonna run over to Waylon's house." I say already
half out the door.

"Well it was nice to see you." She shouts after me, genuinely disappointed.

I stop my sprint mid-step and turn around to go give her a kiss. "I'll be back in 20 minutes." I say with a tender hug, a pang of guilt for the vortex engulfing my life.

Taking a calculated risk with my near future in order to swing by Poppy's house, I scan the innocent, colonial streets for the all too perfecting placed mail truck on my way out of the cul-de-sac. It's nowhere to be seen and I figure if It shows up now, I'll still have 15 minutes as Jesse, our mailman for the last 10 years, makes his way around the same old route from the corner. The short drive is filled with fantasized thoughts of Poppy wallowing in a pit of despair, paralyzed by the reality of life without me. It's unfathomable that she could exist without me. I'll save her from it all, reach my hand over the cliff and pull her back from the abyss. My brain sings a melody about how all will be right with the world as I turn the corner and begin my slow creep down her street. Trees arc over the road, little white picket fences poke playfully above the surrounding hedges, as I hug the soft curve that leads to her place. THERE. She stands in the driveway next to some tricked out little speedster, smiling. Smiling? A recognition of the car - and then I see him getting out the driver's side. Jon Hodgkin, his lanky, do nothing body swinging awkwardly towards her. The pair of them head to toe in black, her long milky legs creeping above thigh highs and disappearing beneath a little black skirt. It's only been a few months since I've seen her, but she has changed. She is gorgeous in a strung out looking way. What is happening right now? Fucking Jon Hodgkin is bad news. Not that I'm good news, but I mean JESUS! I'm me for fuck's sake.

Not wanting her to see me, I hit the gas a little too hard and screech the tires. The sound spins her head towards me. I speed fast around the corner but catch the corner of her eye and watch her through the sad movie frame of my rear view squinting at me in my humiliation.

Around the corner I pull over on the side of the road to sob like a child until some stroller mom glides past me, pulling her kid closer, stranger danger whispering in her mind. The horribleness of it all continues to seep in, soaking me in revolting layers of grime. Quicksand constricts around me, pulling me into a spiral from which I can't pull out. I look for Poppy's hand to pull me from the abyss and only see a light fading away. Undulating waves of darkness and I'm left with my mind a slow helpless drip into sorrow. I throw the car into first and head downtown.

Periodically the scene congeals into something real. People emerge from the walls appearing crisp momentarily and forming solid lines. Everyone is talking, their eyes searching across the rooms for other conversations, antennae raised for something better than where they are. An orchestra of voices engulfing our ears. Music controls their unconscious movements. I can hear everything, know what they're thinking, distant thoughts of subconscious everyone. Silver thoughts fuel us onward and waves of dizziness pass over me as they all begin to dissipate into auras - halos around everything before they disappear again. Back in the universe of my brain, I race through stars unlocking hidden mysteries, vague passages, earth and illusion - a strange life to behold. It takes effort to pull myself back to the outside world and when the focus comes again, it brings with it THE FEAR.

Everyone is a stranger here. Walks of life abound. I realize that I can't trust any of them. Waylon is across the room, silk shirted and smooth, making deals with other silk shirted types. Gold bracelets sneak out below the bottom of their rolled up sleeves, decorating hairy arms and dark skin. They all want to flip the food chain on its head, take their territory and secretly plot the murder of one another, but for now they need one another. I look up at the vents in the wall and become keenly aware that Waylon is still the only occupant in this building. As though I'm in a movie I fly through the lines in the vent and sail through the ventilation ducts to other apartments where I'm certain I find unseen listening devices, hidden cameras and teams of agents. It only makes sense. Waylon escaped them the first time around. Of course THEY are watching. This whole scene is a set up, a set constructed to trap the mice. A Tuskegee experiment. MK ultra. It's like the goddamn Electric Kool-Aid Acid test in here. Voices surrounding. No one is safe. No one is bulletproof. I see Waylon's inevitable demise. I must warn him and make a b-line his way.

"Man. Fuckin A' dude. You got to stop this."

Waylon turns towards me and his eyes register shock and a remote corner of my brain partially realizes, from his expression, that I must look deranged. I brush it off knowing it's only because he does not know the truth I'm about to drop on him.

"They're watching you man." I whisper into his ear.

"Who's watching me?" Further scrutinizing my eyes.

"It's hard to tell which ones, I don't trust any of them, they all look like they're supposed to be here." Everyone's pointing eyes at me, shooting their telepathic laser beams, watching my treachery as I break the news to him, ruining their years of hard work and spying. Everyone is a narc. A strange paranoid power comes over me, a heightened sense of awareness. This is not paranoia, this is reality, I tell myself. Waylon is slipping something into my hand.

"Take this man, you need to come down a bit."

"No, man. I'm fine, for real." I throw the pill down my throat, I mean why not? You know? "I'm just seeing for the first time." I continue to stare down the crowd, looking for the mole or moles, eventually drifting away from Waylon and meandering on wobbly legs back through the crowd. The pill is slowing me down quickly and I'm much calmer about the scenario. Let 'em come get me. Strobe lights flicker against a wall and I follow them down the hallway towards Hayden's room. A blue glow shines at the edge of the darkness, emanating from the same place as the music, pulsing, winding its way through me, luring me closer. I stop at the doorway and through a crowd of writhing bodies I see Hayden DJ'ing on the floor in the corner of the large open space, one headphone on, nodding intently to a blonde diving into his open ear. The music drones above a thick dark beat that replaces my own heartbeat. He mixes in some lyrics from another song.

"Here we are the rolling people, can't stay for long, we gotta go. Come alive with the rolling people. Don't ask why, we just know."

Some forgotten poem runs across my synapses, something about humans falling to earth and remembering heaven. I'm floating on a bed of balloons, lifted by the faint haze in the air. The crowd watches their own scene from above, thinking of themselves in the third person, creating their make believe empires. Needing something to ground me, I back away thinking I'm going to leave the planet for good if I don't stop the drift. A spontaneous combustion will dissolve me into a hovering soul. Consciously, I think about my extremities trying to ensure they're still there. I grip my shoes with my toes and place my hands against the wall as I head towards the bathroom. A guy whom I vaguely know from being around is snorting lines on top of the toilet. He's a tall guy with thinning blond haired greased up into the air. He turns to me wild eyed and welcomes me to his party as though we're long lost friends.

"Try this shit man. Pure Peruvian flake. Oh. Jesus, it's so good. I can barely keep my head from spinning off." He throws his head back, snorts and shakes his head around. There are three massive lines running parallel towards infinity laid out before me. I look at him wordlessly and ask if he's sure.

"Yeah. Yeah. Try it. Go on." Good friends around here.

"Thanks." I say, needing something to lift me out of the coma I'm sinking into. He's skipping out the door before I bend over for the first line. It hits my nose soft as tiny feathers and I know it's the real stuff. Instantly I'm better, finishing up the second line when I hear . . .

"You got anymore?"

Just like my predecessor I'm feeling remarkably gregarious and want to share this new plane to which I've ascended. "Yeah. You gotta try this." I turn towards the voice and see an oddly clean-cut guy looking down at me. He flashes a badge before my face and time stops - still life with jail cells. He says nothing else, looks towards the door to make sure no one else has seen it and puts it away. He stares into my eyes for a second, gives barely distinguishable nod and in a flash of realization I'm validated. THEY are listening. His look tells me I must shut my mouth and never speak of this again. I'm not sure if it's real as he walks out the door, dissolving into the ether. The flake and scene crystalizes the moment, the cosmos finally solidifying before me. An adrenaline dump drops me into the now. I want to rewind it, play it back and make sure what I saw is what I saw. With a force field, I walk back through the crowd, past the unknowing - absorbing. I have an overwhelming compassion for them not knowing the trap they are in. I feel spared from it. Time is at a crawl. I know I should leave and count my blessings - And then I see Poppy standing next to Waylon, his hand on the small of her back as she talks into his ear. It knocks me off balance.

Her eyes are dark beneath some heavy mascara, her hair is greasy and cheeks more sunken than normal. Heroin chic I suppose they'd call it. Waylon gently rubs her back, grooming her to become one of his girls, one of his harem. It takes one to know one, and she's got it bad. I can tell by the way she leans into him that she's begging for some more of whatever it is she's strung out on. I don't know what to do with myself. For an instant I contemplate continuing my way out the door, but any semblance of self control has left me months ago. I stare until she finds me.

"Hunter!!" Her voice slides through the bass lines and stabs my ear. I turn with venom in my blood and pierce her my eyes. There is still a wild light buried in her pupils, a vortex my mind covets, but the rest of her has dimmed somehow. She seems numb to her surroundings as she makes her way towards me. The demons have control of her. Maybe it's me they have.

"Where's John Hodgkins?" I say boldly when she arrives. She recoils as my anger surprises her, knocks her back for a second. She takes the punch like a journeyman boxer and then she springs forward, instantly a prize fight.

"That WAS you! What are doing creeping around my house?"

"What are you doing going around fucking creeps?"

"Fuck you!"

"Yeah whatever." My brief clarity is evaporating into the smoky crack fog of the room. The background extras a motley crew of goddamn Scarface wanna-be's and narc's everywhere, melding into alien creatures. It's like the bar scene from Star Wars – three-eyed bad guys and snout toting drunks

"What am I supposed to do, stay at home in my misery, pull my shades shut and and do nothing?" She yells. I turn back to her, the statement taking a second to process.

"Yes! Yes! You are." I reaffirm. "We had something. How can you deny that?!" People are looking now, vaguely interested, hoping this little scene becomes something more interesting for them.

"You left me outside in the middle of god damn winter."

"Fuck off, you passed out and I was doing everything I could."

"So what? We're we going to do get married or something?"

"Why not?"

"Get off it. I'm in fucking High School Hunter!"

"I was gonna give you everything." Oh Jesus. The emptiness of my words forces me to realize I'm too out of it for this conversation. I know I should stop now.

"What? This?" She seizes the false promise, sinks her teeth in and waves her arm around the room, accusing. My tangential mind easily follows the wave of her hand and I catch eyes with the undercover cop who's now laughing and ribbing with Waylon as though they're old friends. Every sinister connection of the cosmos lights my neurons afire. I'm frozen, unable to trust my own mind. No wonder he was never busted. Goddamn fucking snitch. I'm angry. Angry for Casper sitting wasting away in a cell right now, angry for another half dozen KIDS doing times in various

155

levels of security. It seems as though I'm being set up for something. Like my whole life has been constructed to lead up to a final scene where I'll be presented the answer - Good or bad. I turn back to the love story of the bad B-movie I've walked into and let the arc of my little romance play out.

"This is what you're going to give me?" She has watched my mind wander and leads me back to our conversation where she is the victor.

"Fuck you! You don't even know me. You don't even know what I'm capable of. You have no idea what I'll be." I'm almost muttering to myself. It's ugly and desperate on my end with only a faint belief in my limitless possibilities.

"You're right! I have no idea what you'll be. All I see is what I see." She stares at me with incriminating eyes and I feel the full weight of my nothingness. I feel the dying ember of belief, the blackness of my future.

"If that's not good enough for you then fuck off."

"You fuck off." I'm already heading towards the door, never have even had a fight with her before and now we might as well be strangling one another to match the ferocious intent of our words.

"You have no idea what I want!" She shouts out after me with a million thoughts I've never conceived. I stop and accept the statement, nodding, resolute, trying to remember the promise somewhere in our former lives.

"You're right. I have no idea what you want." I stare at her to let her know that I know her like no one else. She recognizes the juvenile truth of it, a flicker of regret and sorrow spark in her eye. I let it stick, let her see the extent of the gaping axe wound of my soul, let her know that I'm broken and that it's on her. I tell her psychically that she will never find another like me and then I walk out the door with no idea who I am.

Already past the pain, the hurt of it all, there is nothing left but THE SADNESS as I walk down the hallway with no destination in mind. I enjoy it perversely, relish in the emotion, the drama, the finality. It's as though I'm moving through a fucking tar pit, being dragged downed to my destiny for future tourists to stare at my bones. My eyes are heavy, maybe watering, I can't tell. I shake my head to some vague melody of a sad song about how nothing will ever be right with the world and visualize walking straight out the window and down the four stories to my cracked skull on the sidewalk; death, circles spreading out towards the infinite abyss.

The parking lot is a forever expanse of stars rushing overhead as the fruitless search for my keys concludes. My car stares at me, teasing, and the last thing I want to do is go back inside that hollow stage of aliens devouring their own universes, but I'm stranded. I buzz up to Waylon's place a dozen times listening to the wires sizzle, but to no avail. He won't answer even though I know he can see me on the surveillance video. Conspiracies. Am I that fucked up? Out of that whole crowd I'm the one they won't let in now? No. He knows I'm onto him. Fucking rat. I slump down against the bricks and set my resolve to sleep there. The wind blows my hair slightly and lifts my thoughts. I look forward as lights bloom in soft blurred circles. My brain begins to break up into pixelated squares of black and white, spiraling towards the center and I know the tell-tale signs of waning MDMA - although I don't remember eating any of it. Old Cleveland looks down from its squalor, attempting to conceal it's rusty past, and the city seems small. Blues riffs play though my mind as the notion of Chicago springs out of the void, something bigger. The moon rests softly over the crippled skyline illuminating night's starry sheath, the silver city and chameleon lights. I contemplate my all or nothing dive into the risky depths of rockbottomness. The world used to be more interesting when there was an answer in every moment of time. There used to be meaning in every wavy, shadowed line. The realizations having culminated into a conclusion of hopelessness, now I'm not so sure. I stare into the vastness of the fading black.

A faint sensation of motion is tugging me from sleep. Hazy scenery slipping through my eyelids like the flashed scenes of an 8mm home movie. Wind is peeling back my face as I apprehend that my head is hanging outside a car window. I can hear Poppy singing nervously and know I must be dreaming. Slowly though, I wake and turn to see her driving my car, squinting like a grandma at the road, steering too much, a sense of danger bringing me to consciousness. I sit up and she gives me a quick corner of the eye glance, not wanting to break her concentration. I look at the highway in front of us as it weaves from side to side.

"You OK to be driving?" I say, the answer apparent.

"We're almost there." She mutters back as the 1 mile green exit sign for Harbor Bay passes overhead. Cars are flying by us and I look to see she's going 25 mph.

"You need to go faster or you're gonna get pulled over." I say on high alert.

"I can't!" She yells, sounding frightened and I know I just need to hunker down. For another 5 minutes, my eyes try to pry themselves open as I get syrupy flashes of the road. Somewhere in the back of my mind, I numbly pray we make it home. Finally she pulls into my driveway, throws the car into park and lets out a sigh, as do I. The sun is not coming up yet, but I know it must be soon.

"You were sleeping in the parking lot."

"I couldn't find my keys."

"I know." Loud silence washes over us. "Can I come in?"

"Yeah. Of course." We exit the car into the early morning and creep quietly into my parent's house. I stop in the kitchen to see if my report card is laid out on the table covered in tears and count myself lucky when I see no sign of it. Poppy grabs my hand and leads me up to my room. I can't gauge her intent, wonder if I am dreaming and don't know what to make of the situation. Helplessly I follow, ascending into the darkness of the house.

Collapsing onto my bed she joins me and I try to stay awake to search for some resolve. No words come and then I feel her hands on my stomach, reaching down inside my pants. I want to resist, to draw some line. Her lips are on my belly button as I grab her head. "No." I say gently. Images of Jon Hodgkin and Waylon flare-up before my eyes. I don't want to be one of them. She's moving lower and it all feels so good. I remember my anger at her. "No." I say again. I want to love her. I want her to love me. I don't want it to be cheap with her. She's unbuttoning my pants and acting like a sex kitten. I'm so hard and want to consume her but know if it's this, it will always be just this and I will have to share her forever with nameless men. I want her to be different than what she is and love her for it all the same. "No!" I say loudly and push her away, making her feel like a whore. She sits up, obscure in the pitch-black. Dead air swallows the life out of the room. The atmosphere is suffocating leaden.

"Fuck you." She cries and slinks from me.

"Wait." I want to explain myself, my real love for her and reach to grab her but she slaps my arms hard, sobbing. "Fuck you."

She says in a whimper. I know there's nothing left to do as she walks out of my room and closes the door.

The weeping morning comes to my window, leaves turned upwards to catch the sun, light breaking in the violet distance. A million souls awaken while I wait for sleep to come. THE BURDEN steps over the horizon as I lay in my room with books scattered all around me, millions of useless words which mean and say and dream nearly everything. I realize I haven't read anything months and begin trying to write a story in my head. The thoughts scrambled, directionless. Neurons do not connect, sizzling instead in short circuited bursts until everything collapses into itself and I find sleep.

"Jesus Christ it smells like a brewery in here." My dad's voice is the last thing I want to hear right now. He's shaking my leg and I can tell by his tone, he's not happy. A pain runs across my forehead from temple to temple and my eyes are locked shut. "Get up."

I roll over, grunting, wishing him away.

"Get up." He repeats with more force. Deep inside the cloudy, pounding gray fog of my head the alarms go off. I have no idea what time it is and don't know if the mail has yet come.

Regardless, it's late and if hasn't shown up yet, it will soon. He pulls the covers off me and leaves me grasping for their warmth. I curl up into a fetal position as my last vestige of defense, knowing it's no use - his eyes are burning holes in the back of my skull. Surrendering, I roll towards the edge of the bed and onto the floor. There I stay curled on my knees and grab the sides of my head, trying to ease the pain. My father is twenty years sober and has some sympathy for my plight, but not much. "You've got 3 minutes."

"That was a long 20 minutes." My mother says as I enter the kitchen in a daze, fumbling like a zombie towards the coffee through my fogged eyes. It takes me a minute to grasp what's she saying and then I remember I was here yesterday and ran out on her. "Your meal is wrapped up in the microwave." Layers of implied guilt accompany her statement. My dad is sitting at the kitchen table waiting like an inquisitor. I sit down next to him and sip my coffee slowly, scalding the roof of my mouth. I feel gutted, my insides devouring themselves, a stiff pain throughout my torso. Eventually my eyes open as my mother joins us and I see their faces covered in concern. Already I'm waiting for the curtain of night to come to hide me in it's rambling hysteria. I am not made for this . . . this day.

"What is wrong with you?" My dad starts out.

"Whaddya mean?" I can leave whenever I want right? I'm not in jail. For the first time I remember Poppy leaving in the night. My mind starts racing with a thousand thoughts that don't connect and for the first time I realize that maybe there is something wrong with me. *My mind is filled with silvery stars.* I can't quite pull things together.

"What do you mean, what do I mean? Look at you. You're a mess. We had to ask your brothers to leave so they wouldn't see you like this." He stares at me as though that should tell me something. I'm like a Neanderthal with a heavy forehead and a slow moving mind. This is going to go badly. I can feel my nose running and take a large sniff to try and stop it, but it keeps coming. Blood is dripping and pooling onto the kitchen table. Looking up, I cannot explain the amount of bewildered fear that has consumed my parents. I stand up and run to the bathroom, both as a practical action and to escape the situation. They stare at me aghast and turn to one another, as tears begin to form in my mother's eyes.

I'm blowing my nose and filling up toilet paper with crimson evidence. A contorted man stares at me in the mirror. The dark circles and savagery of my face startle me. The slow drip will not stop and so I wad up some tissue, shove it my nose and take as seat on the toilet. I look over at the woodwork where I had carved my brother's name one time when I was pissed at him. I forgot about it until a week later when I heard my mother screaming at him.

"I didn't do it."

"Well who the hell else would carve your name?" Screaming as though there was zero possibility of any other answer. By then I was over my anger and only felt slightly more humor than guilt.

Shaking my head, I put my jaw in my hands and close my eyes. There's no leaving as I need to bide my time here until the mail comes. They would have come out and said it already if they had my grades. Through the wooden blinds I see the sky peaking through the leaves, baby blue shafts of light, and listen closely to their broken voices quivering in the next room. I'll go try to explain to them how I'm not part of the world of wheeled freeways and lottery dreams. I need to prepare for them for the inevitable, that I'll be leaving school and trying to avoid the bosses who laugh their ways through their days saying "Such is life."

"What bosses? When do you work?" my dad is responding.

"Come on Dad. I work." I'm eating leftovers from the night before and we've all avoided the issue of the bloody nose. It's far too real to be real. It's too visceral and their minds won't process. "There's just something different out there for me. I can feel it calling me as if I don't have a choice."

"We always have a choice," he says to me and I wonder if he's right. "That I know," he states emphatically. It's unbelievable

to be trying to have this conversation right now, but I feel as
though I've already jumped through a window from which there's
no turning back. How does Neil Armstrong live the rest of his life
on earth when he's seen it from the moon? I try to collect my
thoughts and come to a coherent point to help them, and myself
feel better. There are grand implications in this simple talk, but I
only know the beginning of the conversation, barely have a grasp
of what I'm after. It's a life changing, altering moment. A
transformation put on a microscope's slide. An unseen fork in the
road, *two roads diverged in a wood* . . . "I'm just onto something
new, that I can't learn in school. I feel like I'm part of a
conversation people have been having for centuries and always
will. Like I'm talking to people in the future and the past." Full
articulation escapes me. They know something's wrong with me
now.

"What are you trying to say? You don't like school anymore?
That's not even an option Hunter." He stares at me as though
THAT can't possibly be my thought process. Tries to beam it into
my third eye.

"I mean, all we have is now." This statement says it all for me.
It should come with thunderclaps and knock them off of their feet.
They should stop and recognize the epiphany of IT - as they never
have before. Gravity should feel heavier - it's revelatory.

"You only think that because you don't know. You could have 80 more years on this planet. You haven't even lived 20. What do you want some factory job?"

"I think I'm gonna be a writer of some sort, a journalist maybe." It seems plausible to me in the moment.

"Oh Jesus Christ." My father throws his head back in disgust. Now he's seen and heard everything. I might as well have told him I was gonna start shitting gold. I stare and wait for some other sort of reaction, some continuation of the conversation, happy that I at least brought up the subject of school, planted that little seed of possibility. From the corner of my eye I watch the front door for signs of the mail. It has to be here by five, two hours at the most, and then I can be gone, somewhere, anywhere, other than here. I am drifting further away from their preconceived notions of what my world would be, drawn by a force away from all I've ever known, becoming something I never understood. I'm thrown back into a sixties photograph of them, black and white, breaking their hearts. I am a mess, an addict of every shade, but somehow it all seems right to me, as though it will lead to something -The delta at the end of the river. I'm worried about the reasoning behind all my reasoning. If only I could tell them the future, share with them the insane reason it's all bright for me. I want to raise a monument to my time spent in eternity, some sort of witness to my existence. In a flash, my darkness seems to be in the past. This could be lunacy;

this is what stepping over to the otherside must be like, "going sane in an unsane universe" as Kerouac said. I hold onto to the notion that someone has felt the same before me. I AM seeing something clearly. The walls hold the reflection of a rose colored sky. Golden balls, like molecules, shift through the atmosphere. A glowing ladder coming down from the clouds, the one born from paintings. The ladder we imagined to be real in heavenly moments of hope. Every thought becomes a movie. I want to play the greatest part in life. The TV from the other room seems to meld with my mind, the voices from it coming from inside my head. A congress of decision makers consults about the reality of reality, this absurd little ball we're on, tiny, so tiny and the mind so large. The collective unconscious says, "Yes. Yes. That's it. Come with us. There are answers here. There is more than the now. The now is all there is. *Everything is sacred, nothing is sacred.*" I seem split, unable to talk to the other me. I can hear myself thinking, but the words are headed nowhere. My parents can sense my mind swirling and have no idea how to approach me. I laugh to myself, only increasing their concern. They are plotting my institutionalization now. They will not have a choice. We always have a choice.

   BBBRRRRRNNNNNGGGG!!

The phone rings to snap me out of it. My mom pushes her aging bones up from the table, thankful to have something to think about other than the deteriorating mind of her eldest son.

"Oh hello Finn." She shoots me a look as though she's talking to someone normal and I should take heed. "How's college treating you? Yeah . . ." Laughing. "I'm sure. I'm sure you're being an angel. Yes. He's here. Sort of . . . I don't know what that means. He's not really himself, why don't you have a talk with him." She's handing me the phone and I take it with a reassuring look to her that it's not all as crazy as it may seem. She sees the sparkle of truth in my eye and appreciates it. Growing up in a house with deaf grandparents allows this sort of communication fairly easily.

"Hello Finn." I say dramatically.

"Oh hello to you sir. What are you doing to your poor parents over there? I'm assuming the mono thing did not work?"

"Uh yeah, not so good." And then pretending I'm listening to him, I quickly devise my escape. "Yeah for sure. If you need my help, I'll come. Absolutely."

"What are you talking about?"

"I can be down there no later than 8 and then we'll load it up tomorrow." "Ahh. O.K. then. I guess I'll see you tonight." Finn laughs, catching on. "We got some good shit brewin' down here. It'll be fun."

I've figure even if I have to wait until 5:00 for the mail, I can make the four-hour drive in three and be down south for some good old boy, redneck fun by the evening. My mind skips forward to the drive, to being out of here - away from the city, away from my parents, away from Poppy, away from the bursting steel to where the land levels out into cornfield rows, away from the scene that is trying to kill me. Plus, I know my parents would rather have me with Finn than anyone else in the world. They'll hope he talks some sense into me and it will relieve the pressure valve of the now for a minute. I see my mother looking at my father, wordlessly asking if they should let me. He looks me in the eye and stares hard before turning to her. "He'll be fine." He says it with implications far beyond the day's events. Like he's done so many times before, he throws down a little stone for me to stand on, a pathway of light to walk through. Just when I'm questioning my answerless future the most, he somehow sees that it will all turn out the end. I am relieved, know he knows, and I believe him.

I'm driving through the rolling hills of southern Ohio, the final haunts of remnant America, past hay barns painted mail pouch red, by tractor graveyards, dull, brown, infested rust, overalls and chicken coops. Soft undulating roads wind past three prisons and

169

numerous new age churches. Passing through it all as a dream, I pop in and out of towns with rundown, pawnshop filled strip malls and dollar discount stores. Rural America, the last refuge from Bradbury's society. Black clad Amish stare at me as from grey bearded interiors of buggies as I whip past, aliens to one another. An airplane leaves it's smoke trail clinging from the sun becoming the prettiest flower I've ever seen. The open roads are smooth and flowing, seemingly twisting and turning with the flowing, racing thoughts of my mind. There's a synchronicity to it as though I have equilibrium with the wind, the speed. I feel a balance behind the wheel, always have. The sun is setting over the trees, burning a hole in the sky and shooting a hazy yellow blast of light through my passenger side window. Beneath my backpack, my unopened report card sits on the seat beside me. Momentary mission accomplished. I race from the consequences, knowing they will eventually catch me.

Pulling into the small town of Athens I remember Finn's directions and drive up to the large brick colonial where he lives. It sits high on a hill with a large wrap around porch that reminds me of a scene from the revolutionary war for some reason. He's sitting on a wicker love seat, shirtless, chiseled, looking like an indestructible statue of David drinking a cheap beer. He lives in a house filled with Division I wrestlers, a volatile mix of testosterone and reckless stupidity. Less than a year ago they would have been my brethren, but now I've become something different, separate. I want to extract him from here quickly and just go hang out, confess my heartbreak, my suspicions about Waylon and whatever else it is that I'm fumbling towards. He's bounding down the steps towards me and a wave of nostalgia comes over me, the familiarity of a shared worldview. It's comforting and I'm hopeful he'll help me make sense of the swirling stream of my emerging actuality.

"Well look who it is. That was fast. Wanted out of town huh?" He throws me a hand slap, fist bump and then goes to tackle me. I fight him off.

"That's right little fucker." I say pushing him away, thankful for the visceral interaction, everything having been so abstract and tangential lately.

"Grab your shit, there's sick boxing matches going on inside, you've got to meet these guys. They're out of their minds." Slinging the backpack over my shoulder I comply, following him up the hill, not wanting to meet anyone. He turns back towards me, smirking, "So what happened with the mono thing?"

"No one bought it man. I pretty sure I'm getting kicked out of school, or at least suspended. I have my grades right here. I haven't opened it yet."

"Oh shit. I'm assuming your parents don't know?"

"Correct."

"Well cheer up man. We're gonna have some fun tonight and figure out that shit later."

In what should be the living room of the house there's a huge crowd of sweating shirtless dudes pressed against the walls as two brutes are swinging haymakers at one another. The big red gloves are splashing blood and spit on the crowd. The men cheer and egg them on, bouncing up and down, getting amped as they await their turn, while a few girls are intermixed sheepishly sipping beer and looking terrified. We mill about the edge of the audience for a couple of minutes until I hit Finn on the arm.

"Come on, I want to open this."

"Well open it then?" He looks at me questioningly.

"I want to steam it open and change my grades."

He looks at me interested. "You're not gonna tell them?"

"Not 'til I have to."

He shrugs his shoulders, leads me into the kitchen, opens the cupboard for a pot and starts boiling some water.

"I've got some shit to tell you." I say as we wait for the bubbles.

"Seems like it." He washes out a solo cup, hands it to me and nods to the keg sitting in the corner of the kitchen. The keg spits out a blast of foam and I'm wondering what he's going to think about my theory of Waylon being a snitch. I'm wondering what I think about it. I'm wondering what I'll do if he believes me.

The steam pulls open the envelope's glue easily and Finn's eyes pop open as he sees five "Failure for Absences" listed out.

"You didn't even go to karate?"

"I've been spending a lot of time at Waylon's," I say as the start of my segue.

"Yeah. It seems like it."

I let the moment slip away and stare at my report card, figuring how I'm going to change it. The type is made up of tiny gray dots from an old printer and I intrinsically know how to alter the page. "You got a pencil?" Thankful my parents don't know how to go online.

Finn leans back in his chair, pulls open a battered drawer and hands me a pencil. Delicately I begin erasing away the ink off the thick grain of the paper and watch with mischievous pleasure as the letters F/A disappear one by one.

"So you and Poppy are done huh?"

"Yeah. I saw her the other night. It was bad."

"Annie says her dad was pisssssssed!" He drags it out for emphasis.

"Yeah. Whatever man. She could've pushed harder. Explained it, or something." My tone gives away my anger. "What's Annie been saying about it?"

"Just that. She didn't have a choice."

"Bullshit." I say, partially jealous that he still has Annie. I feather out the edges of my handiwork to blend it with the rest of the surrounding white on the paper and then I begin meticulously placing lead dots in the shape of my new status report.

B −, C, C +, B, and what the hell an A- in Karate.

I calculate and fill in my new GPA as a 2.47 and figure that's about right - nothing for them to get to excited about and still allow them some real disappointment to better match the tone of reality. It'll simultaneously confirm and relieve their concerns.

"What are you gonna do?" Finn wonders out loud, downing the last of a beer, as he watches me contemplate my deception.

"Get a job I guess." Shrugging, "Gonna have to find a place to live for a while." I pause. "I wanna travel." I say, not knowing whether the thought just occurred to me or not.

"To where?"

"I don't know. I've just been reading a ton and my mind is filled with a million possibilities right now. It's big world out there."

He looks at me hard for a second, understands and shrugs his shoulders - Why not? There are no rules. As he contemplates distant lands, the boxing crowd piles into the kitchen towards the keg, instantly filling the room. "Come on Finnster, let's go raise some shit." Some guy is saying, playfully attacking Finn and shaking him by the shoulders. There's blood trickling from his ear and down the thick veins in his neck. "Fuckin' Millson just got drafted in the first round by the fuckin' Yankees." The whole room erupts into a cheer as a gangly; model looking guy with perfectly coifed hair enters. He's nearly a foot taller than anyone in the room and his abnormally white teeth pop through his perma-wide grin. He throws his arms up towards the sky and lets out a guttural, guerilla like yell, giving praise to his existence. The crowd yells with him as red solo cups fly up into the peeled paint of the ceiling, and beer sprays all over the sweaty bare chests. Caught up in a tidal wave, we roll out of the front door and onto the streets of campus, moving in a pack, our own little Mardi Gras parade, and winding up at an out of the way hole in the wall called the Seldom Inn.

Gray smoke twirls into the dark shadows around the edges of the room, the dingy ceiling collecting murky concerns, a vignetted reality frames the pool tables. A raggedy band is setting up in a marijuana haze. The wave of us crushes the few locals who slide to the edges of the bar to watch drunken brood of masculinity that has just invaded their space. The weathered bartender, slightly pretty, but 15 years past her prime, wears the tales of these smoky nights in the lines of her face. She shares a knowing smile with the owner of the place, whose wrecked face counts the extra drunken money we represent. Knowing we'll eventually be thrown to the streets, they'll be more than happy to deal with the obnoxious stupidity for a couple of hours. There's nothing left for me to do but grab some beer and dive in.

Finn and I are running the table as people keep putting down quarters trying to knock us off. My father spent some time as a pool hustler when he was young and he never let me beat him. It's paid off in hundreds of free beers over the years. Off timed beats run through our shit talking. I'm locked in a moment of clarity, a step into the real world and though I should enjoy it, I'm already thinking of how to blow up the night and go off the rails, or maybe on the rails.

"You get any blow down here?"

Finn is crouched down, lining up a shot. He raises his eyes at me questioningly, with a hint of concern. "I get random drug tests from the NCAA. I can't even smoke a bowl man." He forcefully rams home a difficult shot to make his point. *Can't you just let it go for a night*, he asks with his eyes as he stalks around the table and hovers over his next shot. I'm disappointed and it shows on my face. "Drink your beer." He admonishes me. I finish off the frosty mug with a big gulp.

"You want another?" I ask and he raises his eyebrow at my dumb question. "Well run this shit then." I order as he gives a confident nod. I walk over to the bar and order a couple of beers, taking a shot of whiskey for myself. Finn's buddies are celebrating with their star pitcher. I get my shot and yell, "Cheers to Millson."

"CHEERS!!" They erupt.

"Let's get fucked up!" I yell as if they need help.

"YESSSS!!" They yell back, downing their beers and shots. It's all it takes for me to ingratiate myself with this clan. I get a slap on my back and head towards Finn. He's chalking up his stick as the next challenger racks the balls.

"You been doin' a lot of blow huh?"

"I haven't been buying it or anything."

"Well you don't have to when you have Waylon." He leans down over the break and cracks the rack. "Solids." He calls across the table after sinking one of each. "What's that shit you were saying about him being in on something?" He says it half interested and marches towards his next shot.

"Yeah man, I don't know if I'm paranoid or what, but there's some suspicious shit going on his place." I embellish the scene a bit, "Some dude flashed his badge there at me the other night and told me I needed to keep my mouth shut".

"What?" He says disbelievingly.

"There are so many shady people running around there. A lot of gold chain wearing, Middle Eastern dudes, ball players, junkies, local rock celebrities . . . I've seen people selling machine guns for Christ's sake. You go to the bars and they don't even serve alcohol, its just pre-opened water bottles they give away and everyone rolls all night. They lace the water with MDMA."

Finn flashes a look at that, not knowing whether to believe me.

"Then this dude that flashed me his badge was all cozy with Waylon, laughing and shit, just staring and observing all these different people. I felt like a rat in a cage, like it was some sort of experiment or trap or something."

"Yeah. It sounds like paranoia to me."

"Dude he lives in that building with no one else in there. How the fuck did he make it through the whole WEB arrests? He's so dirty and they don't have anything on him? I don't buy it. I think he made a deal with someone." I want him to believe me, so I try to hit home. "Now fucking Casper is in the federal pen."

"That was is own doing."

"Even so . . . I don't know man, it's hard to articulate. They know he was running the shit and now he just sets up downtown and is given free reign to start a little cocaine empire? You think the feds just walked away from him. If he's not in on it, you know they have to be watching him. He'd have to be busted by now."

"You seem pretty irate for someone who's been living it up over there."

"This thing with the cop just happened the other night. I saw it all so clearly. Maybe I'm crazy. I don't know. Poppy was there too, so that fucked me up."

Finn misses a shot and sidles up to me, ignoring the whole Poppy conversation.

"Well what if that is the case? What if he did make a deal? What are you gonna do about it?" The band is looking fairly pathetic, putting on Rastafarian heirs and playing a bad cover of a Marley song. Our opponent has a clear run of the table, if he doesn't blow it. "I mean you want to go after him or something."

"I don't know. I mean if he cut a deal, he fucked up a bunch of people's lives."

A drunken guy rolls up next to us, leaning a little too close. "I am a black belt, a marine and I'm in the mafia." He says to us, slurring, with a hint of hysteria. He can barely stand up and his veiled threat is empty. "I've done it all a million times, but comes a time when it must be done." He continues as our opponents sink the 8 ball. Finn and I put our cues down and walk away from him to go find a spot at the bar.

"You know I'm not buying the whole Waylon confidential informant, lab rat thing right?"

"I don't know if I'm buying it. It was just a moment. I can't put my finger on it, but something's not right."

"That I'll buy." He says pensively over his mug. We both sit and think about what that may be for a minute.

"It's early man, but I don't think beer is gonna cut it for me tonight."

"We'll get into some trouble. I got a treat coming for us."

I perk up instantly. "Yeah? What kind of treat?"

179

He wants to keep it a secret but can't contain himself. "There's this dude." He giggles. "He's in med school training to be a neurosurgeon down here. Just transferred in. He got kicked out of Case Western for making his own acid up there."

"And they let him in here?"

"They only had suspicions because he booby trapped his stash chemically or something, so they asked him to leave. Anyways, this shit is amazing." He gives me a shit-eating grin. "He should be here in about 10 minutes."

"Thank god. I thought you had gone straight edge on me there for a minute with the looks you've been throwin' at me." I say laughing.

"I haven't. But that doesn't mean you shouldn't." He replies, half joking.

20 minutes later this normal looking jock dude comes bouncing into the bar with wild eyes. He instinctively sees Finn and heads our way.

"What is going down man?" He says and it's instantly apparent he is long gone on the product. "I am on a wave dude, on a wave. Like riding on top of it all." He slides his hand forward slyly to show it's all smooth sailin' and lays a couple of tabs in Finn's hands. "On the house man. I need some friends to join me on the next level." His smile is encouraging and we both want to ascend quickly. Finn hands one to me.

"Hunter meet Burke. Burke, Hunter."

"Nice to make your acquaintance." He smiles with a feigned accent.

"Likewise," I say, playing along.

He turns to the bartender, "Three O.J.'s please."

She looks at him quizzically and he just nods affirmation. Turning to us, he says, "It helps get through the turbulence."

A few minutes later the room turns about us and strange angles twist through the tunnel of my mind - stepping into the fourth dimension or some such shit. Finn and I give each other a sideways glance and our newfound guide, Burke lets out a little laugh. "It's good."

I need to keep my head down for a bit and let the floor ground me. I don't want to look up as a faint mixture of voices blends with the music. I know now what he meant by turbulence and I ride through it until I just start laughing hysterically at the absurdity of it all. Finally I'm able to look up and Finn does so at the same time. An hour could have passed. Burke just nods and smiles.

"Welcome."

"I need another O.J." I believe comes out of my mouth.

"Coming right up." He says turning away, "Barkeep, 3 more O.J.'s please."

We drink them and stand with the feeling of levitation. We're just starting to take off and I look around at people ordering drinks and trading dollar bills, the movement of the hands neatly wrapping up the knowledge of centuries.

"I think we're up." Finn says weakly, motioning for the table. He had put some quarters down after our last defeat and the same two guys have the table. I bust out laughing and we walk over to the table. Finn has trouble sticking the quarters in the slots and finally kneels down and focuses all of his efforts on the task. I can't take my eyes off of him. He keeps racking the balls in the wrong order until one of the other guys, annoyed, offers to do it for him. The rack cracks and they sink nothing, but Finn and I are frozen.

"You gonna shoot at something or what?"

Without talking we put our cues down on the table and turn to leave the bar. Burke is already at the door waiting for us as though he ordered us to leave or at least knew we would. We step outside into the night and as the door closes, the rowdiness of his friends closes with the door and turns into muffled murmurs. The night air is fresh on us - a new world emerged. At the end of the walkway that leads out of the bar is a little hatchback running on the street. Burke walks up and looks in the passenger side window.

"The keys are in it." And without a second thought he steps back and karate kicks the window in. "Who wants to drive?"

"I will." Shrugging my shoulders as though it was the most normal situation in the world. I walk around to the driver's side and open the door that was unlocked. Burke starts laughing as he sweeps the shattered glass off the seat. I throw the car into drive and with *crystal vision* peel off down the street. Burke is rattling off a monologue about serotonin receptors and dopamine production. He tells us how he is trying to perfect a combination of molecules he's convinced will take humans to another level of consciousness. I realize quickly that he is no flake and has solid backing to his theories - chemical equations and processes. He talks about how the apes started eating Psilocybin mushrooms and that became the missing link in the evolutionary chain.

"Kubrick knew man. Kubrick knew," he's saying. "That whole thing with the apes and their tools screaming at the monolith. He was saying it all right there on film. There is no time man. You know the Hopi Indians don't even believe in time? I mean who made this date, this year? Chopped it up into minutes and seconds? Huh? It's so artificial. I was on a Navajo reservation once and the chief was telling me he was a shape shifting, skin-walker. I was like, yeah whatever and then I saw him, right before my eyes man, turn into a crow. It was some Carlos Castaneda shit."

"What were you on?" Finn asks, getting straight to the point.

"Peyote man. But, what the fuck? That's reality too. A damn good reality I might add." And with that he busts out laughing so hard that it becomes a crazily infectious hysteria and we're all crying, tears streaming down our faces. I squint to try and maintain some view of the road, but the moisture is throwing paths of light every which way and all the colors of the world are turning into neon tracers, worming at warp speed through a neighborhood with sleeping houses. We're racing towards shiny oblivion. With each deliberate turn I find myself waiting for the world to become angelic. I whirl down the street that winds through the center of town and instinctively start popping up onto the lawns and surfing long, drifting glides dangerously close to front porches. The future is right there, lingering before my mind and I feel as though I can break through. I'm trying to catch the present as it continually moves out of reach, rapidly falling into a former me, yet continually constructing who I am. Faster.

"HOOOLLLLY SHIIIIITTTTT!" Burke is screaming at the speed of it all. Our lives are coming at us in melting fragments. We're about to pop through the threshold when CRRRASSSH!!!!! I nail a stop sign. The little car bends the metal post of the sign and slides up it, coming to a rest with its front tires dangling in mid-air. After a moment I snap out of it, throw the car in reverse and gun it, but the front wheel drive tires race futilely above the ground. We all whip our heads towards each other and fly out of the doors, instantaneously hurtling through the neighborhood. Burke takes off in the opposite direction from us, purposely, and we never look back. I'm almost certain he was real. Finn and I are flying through backyards, up and down little gulleys and in five minutes we're a mile away, resting on hill overlooking the little subdivision we just terrorized. The adrenalin rushes back out to our limbs and we remember we have maybe another 10-hour trip left to go. We stand to continue our journey as red and blue lights converge from all directions on the spot we just left. Barren limbs crack the dirty purple sky above us, as the silent tender call of the moon pushes us onward.

Finn knows where he is and takes us on a circuitous route back to the center of campus. We walk behind houses; shrouded in trees that breathe in the air, pulsate in the night, capillary branches feeding the earth. Shadows stretch their fingers across the hills as we pass by separated families, locked in heads of their own making. Linen mothers nestled in their hobbled basements playing the part, arms wrapped tight to destroy the alienation in our Alien nation. Slowly we make our way to the neon OPEN signs of town. The first place we see is a small church that has a warm inviting light poking misty rays above the entrance. As we draw closer we hear a choir singing and are helplessly drawn into a midnight mass as though we have no choice. It seems to be the diamond future drenched in sun. The light bathes us as we enter. A pastor is center stage, swaying back and forth, leading a choir of a dozen robed singers. I veer towards a back pew and sit down, mesmerized, not giving Finn a second thought as he walks methodically straight up the center aisle towards the pastor. Eventually it dawns on me that he is going to talk to him, mid-song. It seems angelic. Slowly, the pastor realizes it as well and they lock eyes. Finn is standing beneath him now; a couple of steps below the altar slash stage. The pastor's efforts to shoo him away are useless. Finn starts talking and I'm trying to decipher the meaning of it when I hear a growling next to me. There's a ragged man lying on the bench contorted as though afflicted with some sort of muscular disease. His hands and feet twist weirdly at the joints and he oscillates between complete prone rigidity one moment and a curled fetal position the next. I notice other disheveled men and women occupying the rest of the back pews as he continues to growl at me. I see others disappearing down a set of stairs in the corner of the church and somewhere in the back of my mind it registers that this must double as a homeless shelter. The man is growling directly at me, trying to communicate, but I'm unsure whether I'm hallucinating or not. He seems to want something from me, but I have nothing to give and I start to slide away from him back towards the aisle. I'm walking backwards out of the church, the same way I came in. Finn is engaged in conversation with the pastor, who is smiling from ear to ear and the choir carries on with wry smiles, watching the two of them. From a hundred yards away I make out a few of Finn's words "Future dreams and spotlights."

The choir watches me as I go backwards through the door, as though I never came.

It's a singular journey now as I head straight down the middle of the main street. People are piling out of the bars, laughing and cavorting, moving in packs. I am separated from it all, a floating apparition in their world. My eyes are wide open and carrying me along. As though magnetized I walk alone with the night towards the highest hill in town, listening to the sewers speak, having conversations with the wind as the road rises and leads to a wooded trail. There's a fog in the air, resting in the valleys, all the flowers seemingly turn to stare as I walk the path. There's no turning back, and all the questions that I've asked, paint the night black. The trail opens up to a clearing that overlooks the whole town. I can see for miles in all directions as the sky bursts into a million stars to mix with the ones revolving in my head. The world rushes about my anchored feet and I am at peace. Useless notions are swept into the void; fresh streams of consciousness that will vanish, as always, like myriads before. I lock my stare upon a star and drag the end towards me, gripping infinity in my hand, balling it up in my fist and throwing it away into a corner to be forgotten. I want to scream, take a bite out of the sky, ravage something, anything. Floating. Answerless, as we all must be. I remember a Native American tale about the blue coyote that lived between worlds, and for a moment, I am a blue coyote. There's a marching band somewhere and it's all just endless nonsense in the great forever game. Words can never come close to describe, we forget.

I lay for hours in visions that race across my eyes, awake and dreaming. Energy springs from the ground, reaching its green hands to hold me until the clouds, hung on strings, paste pink collages on the orange horizon. I rise, returning to myself, the same as before, only filled with the knowledge that we can never know. I brush myself off and walk through the soothing arms of the sleeping town. As I approach Finn's house I can see him coming towards me and know he came from the hill that rises behind him. We both arrive at the bottom of the slope below his house, parallel travelers. Wordlessly we walk towards the door, dragging our dreams into the day as the sky creeps over us in pastels, lurid ocean blues.

I awake to find another month gone. Freshly washed clothes hang around me on clotheslines, another load is rumbling around in the washer next to my bed. The scent of mildew wafts in from the corners of the basement I've made into a makeshift room, it mixes with the moisture clinging to the cinder block walls. Regretfully and with much struggle, I pry myself from the sheets and roll myself sideways, putting my feet onto the cold cement floor. Zombie-like with fogged eyes, I fumble out into the next room which acts as a tavern, complete with a bar and foosball table. I notice someone crumbled up on the couch and the ancient T.V. is playing Pink Floyd's "The Wall" on repeat. I make my way towards the stairs and up into the kitchen, piled high with dirty dishes and overflowing garbage cans. The coffeemaker is off, but there's a cups worth caramelizing in the carafe. I pour some, pop it into the microwave and take it to the living room. The house is silent. Everyone, but the body downstairs, must be at class. I curl up in a blanket and sip my coffee, trying to wipe the sleep from my eyes and slip through the threshold of a new day. As always, I'm watching a hind sighted movie of my life play out on the back of my eyes, the past a crystal ball predicting my future. One cup of coffee is not nearly enough to get me going, so grabbing a book and a notepad, I get dressed and head to the local coffee shop.

Outside the door I'm momentarily cleansed by a bursting blue sky. The walk through the silent afternoon is crisp and I step knowing something must come from these ramshackle days. The coffee shop is abuzz with all sorts; business men on calls - actors of the suburban stage getting paid for time, vagrants nursing free refills, students being studious, hippies, clad in disarray, lurking - plotting idealized worlds, staring straight down with a smile. Conversations are colliding as baristas steam their faces over cappuccinos. My eyes scan the room for an angel as the world rushes by in a timid imitation of life. A loneliness infiltrates my mind, a space between touch, a waning second where our eyes meet and all the judgments of the world come crashing in. I take my coffee and pull up a chair in a distant corner, set to observe and think and write. It's become my pretend existence, an occupation in my mind. At last I don't feel like nothing like I did there for a minute. My notebook is filled with discarded, scattered memories, worries a splendor and trifle occurrences. I want every moment to be a mind exploding revelation of truth. The desire is impossible to shake, days are lighting the fuse. To make it in this world one must believe they are a genius, yet know only fools occupy this land. The seconds inch along, signaling my inevitable departure from this place. In a hazed, dreamy way, there is a longing for the truth of the blues, sadness haunts of dank winter walks. A cute girl keeps stealing glances at me as hair falls into her eyes. She throws her head back, laughing at the ceiling, letting me know that all is right with her world, but nothing comes of it except for the corner of the eye glimpses. I look out the window at invisible stars burning in someone else's night. I can hear summer rolling in the distance, the daydream of winter gloom.

The hours pass and eventually I leave, walking out helpless beneath the sky turned orange and the trees, black as eternity, cover me in Halloween night. I embrace the solitude, the grated sidewalks, storybook houses lining the rows and the mind seems to know. I want to write it all down and try not to forget the waning thoughts left on the side streets of America. The brittle trees are just beginning to bud, stirred occasionally by the wind. The air has flown through time and seen it all. I can see my house in the distance - a car in the driveway. I think my mind is playing tricks on me as I draw closer and realize its Poppy's.

My pace slows as I take some deep inhales to calm myself. I don't know what to feel about it. The lights burning through the front windows reveal nothing. With a great deal of trepidation I step towards the front door, my heart falling into my stomach. I walk in and see my roommate, Joe, giving glasses of water to Poppy and Annie. Both of them have their knees to their chest, rocking back and forth. They are sobbing hysterically, their faces a puffy red as though they've been crying for hours.

"We didn't know what to do. Your mom didn't know what to do." Annie blubbers. Poppy sits next to her with vacant eyes, sunken in their sockets, staring out lifelessly.

"About what?" I'm terrified. What could be happening?

"We couldn't find you all day." Annie looks at me, pleading for something.

"What? Tell me. What?"

"It's Finn. Finn died in a car crash last night."

For a moment I'm frozen, everything draining out of my body until I drop to the floor. "No. No. No . . . " I say endlessly, shaking my head in my hands. "Noooooo!" I scream into the carpet and Joe comes up and puts his hand on my back as I start balling. I'm hit by dark blasts of reality, my mind's cavity blackened. It's empty as all must be.

Leap

The sun busies itself painting a fresh fresco sky as we drive towards the cemetery. It's now eight in the morning and five hours ago I had myself nearly fooled into sleep. I saw him in the hallways as I roamed through the dark house all night. I watch school bus windows catch reflective waves as kindergarten plucks kids from the nest, left wide-eyed and afraid as mothers become a spot on the horizon. Drifting through the world, past the ignorant cars, filled with eyes that will never know our pain. Exhaust pipes throw their thick shadows. My bat and glove are locked in nostalgic closets, commemorating another passing year. I look at my town through the eyes of stranger and think that years mean nothing without the people to watch them swim by.

The cemetery is plush from spring rains, bounding green on rolling hills. The long line of black cars rumbles softly over the gravel roads. Flowers linger, rising out of the trimmed scenery, feeding on tears. Solemn faces of grandparents creak out of back seats while hushed whispers console. In the front row I see Finn's father looking up towards the heavens, the clouds draining questions from his eyes and a thousand of the sky's mocking replies. I sit down behind him and Finn's mom, between my parents, their hands holding mine. The wind brushes gently past me. The world is serene in grief for a moment. Somehow, somewhere along the way I have found a belief in something. An energy. The blue light. It comforts me now in cascading waves of stillness. If all the madness is pervasively black and right, why shouldn't I leave it behind and leap into the light? My head rises above it all and I breathe in the air. I have seen things. I am confident in my knowing that this is not all. A priest approaches the casket and I can hear a choir singing, a dozen swaying smiles from that night not long ago. Things change, this we know.

"Good morning." He begins. There are whimpers and wails. I feel a tear rolling down my cheek and miss by best friend. I hear him laughing, sitting besides me in my passenger seat wearing a Viking helmet. A million memories play out inside the domed theater of my mind. I try not to think about him flying out the passenger window of some car and over the side of a bridge 200 feet down. I think about the light. I think about it all NOW.

The service is in motion, words sailing on currents past me. I look around the crowd and see Waylon a couple of rows back. Without the night to hide his features, I can see his greasy skin, pocked with acne from the steroids he's started taking. He is hardened and stares straight ahead. But he loved Finn as I loved Finn. We catch eyes and I push back my thoughts about him. We share only a nod of understanding. Casper had called collect from jail this morning. I spoke, filled with regret for my self-involved lack of communication with him. I told him how well Finn was doing in school, told him of our night in the universe. He had been moved to a minimum-security prison for his good behavior and they let him have his guitar. I told him I had started playing as well and we traded blues riffs and Dylan songs we knew. We hatched plans to play together one day.

"Everything is so unreal." He said as we hung up the phone. I stared out the window.

Annie sits in front of Waylon, a mass of curly hair hunched over, shaking violently with sobs. Her mother rubs her shoulders and looks off vacantly. Everyone is on their own. Finn's mom reaches her hand backwards towards me and I take it with the most unmanageable feeling I have ever known. We can only look at one another for a heavy second before we both begin crying madly. It does not end.

A couple of Finn's cousins shovel symbolic mounds of dirt onto the casket, their arms barely able to move as they sob for the gentle, playful soul we all loved and admired. We're a mass of black sparrows spreading out along the ground, away from the scene and towards our cars. Heavy clouds are filling the air, the day becoming an appropriate gray. I'm staring at my feet, plodding along on legs I don't feel, when I feel a hand on my shoulder. I turn to find Poppy's dad looming over me.

"I'm very sorry Hunter." He says sincerely.

"Thank you." I say, realizing that I have not seen Poppy, that she has not crossed my mind.

"Can I talk to you for a minute?"

I have not slept in over a day, have been crying for an hour straight, nothing left in me and whatever he wants will surely push me over the edge into some wilderness I only vaguely sense exists. I feel as though I can legitimately tell him "Not now", but sensing my hesitation, he continues.

"It's Poppy. I need your help." Her foreboding absence now riddles my mind with a string of horrible possibilities, rapes, overdoses and a dozen other unimaginable things.

"Sure." I answer as he leads me away from the flood of mourners. We walk up a small rise, stopping out of earshot from anyone. A line of trees stretches behind him as he drops his head lower.

"We had to put Poppy away."

"What do you mean?" I say after a moment of incomprehension.

"She needed to go into the hospital." His speech is slow and pained.

"She's had some sort of break from reality. They've got her on medicine now to try and help her. But I don't know. It's been a couple of days and she's not doing well." He breaks down crying and begins stammering. "I'd like for you to go see her. I don't know if it will help. But I don't know what else to do."

I'm looking for the light. My mind will not work. Rain begins to fall.

There's a long corridor in the center of the state mental hospital through which I'm being led to a cafeteria. Eerie noises and screams come from random directions, echoing off the cement walls. I realize quickly this is no cushy rehab or pleasant vacation place for some rest; it's seemingly haunted by ghosts of the living. An orderly marches on ahead of me, long accustomed to way gone cases, as I try to keep up. A feeling of dread gives way to paranoia. I give a glance at the visitors pass clipped to my shirt, making sure this is not some elaborate ploy to have me locked up.

We enter the small eating area that's littered with a half a dozen tables. Relatives sit beside patients in varying degrees of catatonia. No one eats the food in front of him or her. Families stare hopeless, searching for words.

"Take a seat there and I'll go get her." The orderly tells me coldly, giving a nod to an empty table in the corner. It's next to a window and the sun's rays catch the floating dust in a soft parade. I sit, trying not to make eye contact with anyone. Wallowing in the sense of shared, inescapable pity blanketing the air, I keep my head down.

A few minutes later a door opens across the room and Poppy comes shuffling slowly through it, her head down, dark hair hanging limply in front of her eyes. She wears only a surgical robe, barely tied at the back, and a pair of hospital issued socks. She is moving aimlessly away from me until the orderly, as though he's turning her towards a piñata, spins her in my direction. Her shuffle slows further as I stand to hug her. She is frightened like a small child hiding behind their mother's leg. Wrapping my arms around her frail body she feels as empty as a paper bag. Her arms hang listless at her side and then a wave of small convulsions begins, little earthquakes of her shattered soul. I can feel her pointy bones vibrating. I squeeze her tightly, running my arms up and down the muscles along her spine, wanting to be comfort, wanting to be all she will ever need. I want to let her know that everything is temporary, except for us. As though it never happened, she stops shaking as quickly as she began and pulls away from me. I try to look at her eyes through the greasy strands of hair. They are vacant, debilitated, unable to see anything before her.

"Poppy?"

No response.

"It'll be ok." I bend my knees to try and look at her, arms on her shoulders, and know that it's not the truth. Something has cracked, split and is unable to come back to the world. She is not here. I help her gently to a seat and stroke her arm with all the love I have for her.

"You're dad tells me you're doing better." I say in an attempt to be strong, trying not to cry. "Can I get you anything?"

"I don't know." She says meekly, staring through me.

"Something to drink?"

"I don't know."

Needing to escape from the dark void for a moment, I stand and head to the soda fountain. Hiding my tears, I spray some lemonade into a paper cup. To bide time, I grab a blueberry muffin, wrapped in plastic, exhale deeply and turn to her. There she languishes. The soft wind outside makes the shadows of leaves dance across her. Her beautiful, wild eyes that once danced as well are now gone. A hollow gray stare that opens to an empty chasm has taken its place. She sits in a box of shiny sunshine dust. I walk slowly towards her, not wanting to be another one of the silent tables surrounding us.

"Take a sip." I put the lemonade down in front of her.

"I don't know." She repeats.

I am on the *verge of disaster*. Through the window, between the scattered clouds of everyday, a hole burns in the sky. It leads to something more. I want to slide through it to look back on the world, to remember the life we once knew. We sit for years as the families around us begin to say their sad goodbyes, hanging heads and shuffling feet disappearing into various silences.

We're the last ones there when the orderly pops his head in between some swinging doors. "Five minutes left for visitation."

I sit thinking of all the things I wanted for us, to be a poem to her as she was to me. Nothing will change anything. I never want to say goodbye. All the possibilities drift through the walls into the either. I desperately want there to be a reason for everything, a reason to have met and loved, but maybe the world does not work like that. She shudders as though coming back to the world for a moment. Remembering I'm there, she looks up at me and I see it. The white point of light in her eyes, the glowing tunnel that has always connected us. She sees it too and we focus hard on the pinpoint glimpse of hope. I hang onto with everything I have in my drained soul, hoping that she will crawl from the dark rooms in her mind calling her. Her lips rise at the corner and she knows once more. Then it's gone. She is not meant for this place. Her face drops, her mouth sags and with a final dousing of the light, she turns away, afraid of the good, not trusting that anything can ever be right. I've lost her forever to the space inside. She is still an angel who held hands with me, on the ride, for a brief speck of time.

From across the yard I can see the hard, crusted wrinkles around the eye of the bird. Nearly imperceptible streaks of shining gold and blue slide down into the circular canyons of its reptilian features, now hidden mostly by feathers. Head sideways, it stares back at me like a Cyclopes. Life is amazing. It's so apparent that they were once dinosaurs and now fly above us with a freedom we may never know. Thousands and thousands and thousands of years. How can I truly mean something in the face of all this time? My car is in the driveway, packed with meager belongings; a suitcase full of clothes, a sleeping bag and pillow, and my $50 dollar guitar. I close my eyes and let the sun burn red on the back of my eyelids, watching blood vessels turn into moving microcosms. I picture the infinite inside of me and knowing I am just part of it makes me feel as large as the universe itself. The bottom is three weeks past. I remember the devil coming out of the walls. I remember imaginary wars for my soul as the alcohol and drugs seeped out of my skin. I know I will never go through the shaking, heart racing terror again.

We were all just foolish, innocent kids running barefoot through the grass, clutching the days by the clouds. The golden, skipping flashes were eternal, a laughter so light. But now I must become a warrior and lean into this life with a vengeance.

Everything is fleeting. I know that it is only me. No one else is coming to save me - and I'm okay with that. You have to be ready to struggle, to fight. I pull away and start down the road. It's hard to describe the tangential thoughts that run through a scattered mind and all the dreams that are hatched in the spaces between. I dream of dreams coming true. Now I can only escape and go into the massive dome of the unknown and see for myself. Plodding onwards, I slash my machete at the sunbeams. These are the words I shall leave, the words of pen and paper memory.

About the author:

Brian Fox is a writer, producer and director living in Chicago, with a feature film and dozens of commercials to his credit. He currently works at Leo Burnett Worldwide as a Senior Producer creating commercials for clients such as Sprint, Samsung, Nintendo, Coke and many others. He spent many years in Chicago as a musician and graduated from Columbia College Chicago's film program. His spare time is spent writing screenplays and producing independent film projects.

Connect with Me:

Follow me on Instagram: http://instagram.com/buddhaloop

Follow me on Twitter: http://twitter.com/buddhaloop

Check out my work: http://iamsciencefiction.com

Thank you for reading my book.

If you enjoyed it, won't you please take a moment to leave me a review at your favorite retailer?

Thanks!

Brian Fox